SATURDAY SANTA

The Canyon Club – Book 3

Kate Moore

PRAISE FOR THE CANYON CLUB

The Loner

"Kate Moore has won me over and I really look forward to reading more books in this series and anything else she writes."
~Confessions of YA and NA Addict

"The characters are very lovable. It is a must read and if you love reading about people who try to claim their love then this is the book for you."
~Summer's Book Blog

"Engaging, sympathetic protagonists, a well-rendered supporting cast, and a satisfyingly sigh-worthy love story at the center of a well-paced plot get this planned trilogy off to a superb start."
~Xpress, Library Journal

Golden Boy

"Well written. It was full of action, drama, and romance. I absolutely loved the ending." ~Boundless Book Reviews

"I'm a Southern California native, and this book took me right back to my old stomping grounds. I've read many of Kate's books, and this one is among my favorite."
~Bay Area Book Guy

"Ms. Moore tells a compelling story, but my favorite thing about Golden Boy is the beautiful and unexpected ways she puts words together. I found myself stopping to re-read the lovely descriptions that brought me wholly into the story. I enjoyed Golden Boy very much and Kate Moore is now on my list of favorite authors."
~Night Reader

www.BOROUGHSPUBLISHINGGROUP.com

SATURDAY SANTA

ISBN: 978-1-953810-85-4

For Loren, again and always

ACKNOWLEDGMENTS

Many readers are familiar with the popular song refrain about "silver bells" and Christmas time in the city. No one, I think, has written a great Christmas song about a mall. And yet, for me and my children, the mall at Christmas was a wonderland. A bustling, decorated place, a treat for the senses, full of lights and music, tall candy canes, and Santa's workshop.

I began writing *Saturday Santa* as Christmas, 2020 approached with retail as we'd known it shut down. In those dark days, it was comforting to bring back Christmas 2015 in the lives of my characters from the Canyon Club series—*The Loner*, Will Sloan and his Annie Wilde, and *Golden Boy*, Josh Huntington and Emma Gray, and Emma's son Max. And now the story of Jack Ryker, a most unlikely hero, and the ordinary woman who changes his life, Mari, Lynch.

The book would not have been written with a "Yes, we want it," from my publisher, Boroughs Publishing Group, or without my agent's unflagging support.

Though we could not meet in person, the Mill Valley Library writers meet-up group, carried on in Zoom meetings. The insights of my fellow writers, who are also savvy readers, spurred my imagination and guided me away from serious plot holes. My long-time brainstorming friends, Barbara Freethy, Barbara McMahon, Candice Hern, Carol Grace, Diana Dempsey, and alas, now no longer with us, Lynn Hanna, all made valuable suggestions. Jorge Rodriguez, a former teaching colleague, and now Director of Teaching, Learning, and Equity at Mid-Peninsula High School, was my go-to source for video games.

I must thank my husband for bringing me that perfect morning cup of coffee and allowing me to give the first moments of my day to pen, paper, and imagination.

All characters and places are fictional. Any mistakes in understanding Jack's medical condition and the traditions of the U.S. Marine Corps are my own.

I hope you enjoy Jack and Mari's journey to the first day of happily ever after and a brief reunion with other Canyon characters you've met in the series.

As Christmas 2021 approaches, I wish everyone blessings and joy.

SATURDAY SANTA

Chapter 1

November 2015

From his living room window two stories above the Strand, Jack could see the woman coaxing her reluctant companion along the public walkway. The Strand, a wide, smooth concrete ribbon, ran from the edge of the Palos Verdes hills to the northern end of the South Bay beach towns, passing in front of miles of multi-million-dollar beachfront houses. Jack leaned forward slightly in his chair, and Soldier, the black dog at his side, raised his head, instantly alert to his needs. He couldn't hide anything from Soldier.

Mid-November was not exactly winter but a milder form of LA's perpetual summer with shorter days and cooler temperatures, and even one brief rainfall last week.

Jack had taken possession of the beach house in July and he was familiar with the woman's almost daily performance and her tactics for handling the old man beside her. Jack figured she had a specific goal in mind, a corner to be reached on these outings. He guessed from the timing of her first appearance and the interval before her return that the turnaround point was a park a few blocks north of his place.

A strong afternoon breeze shook the old guy, to whom she gave her arm, and it blew her dark brown hair wildly about her face. The old man had to be fifty years her senior, with thick, short-cropped white hair and a stoop in his wide shoulders. He had the brown and weathered look of a man who'd spent years in the sun, and his clothes came straight out of old salt casting. Khaki pants hung on his lean frame sagging over his boat shoes. A frayed and faded pink knit collar stood up around his thin neck, and one elbow poked through the arm of his dark blue sweater with some yacht club burgee on the breast. His lurching, uncertain gait required constant adjustment on the woman's part. That and the old man's tendency to balk at Jack's house as if he refused to take another step.

He did it again, stopping below Jack's window, steadying himself by grabbing hold of one of the thick glass panels separating Jack's patio from the passing crowd. The woman turned to the old man with a smile. She had pink cheeks, rounded features, and coffee-colored eyes, with long dark lashes. From the look on her face, Jack imagined her saying some light, bright, encouraging thing. She didn't lose her temper. Jack knew he would, but she never did. Her patience with the old man pissed off Jack every time.

Watching her made him tighten his hold on Soldier's nape, who tensed in response and Jack carefully relaxed his hand. He didn't want to confuse his most reliable ally.

It wouldn't be hard for Jack to find out who she was. He had the resources and the connections. One of his security cameras had no doubt already recorded her image. He could scan the thing and run it through his facial-recognition databases. Hell, he could send one of his security guys down to the Strand this minute while she and the old man lingered in front of his patio. A little muscle from one of his guys might scare her off, keep her from stopping in front of his place, and he would be spared another day of watching her.

Not what he wanted. Not yet. He could, if he chose, get up out of his chair with Soldier's help, and make his way to the elevator he'd installed. He could descend to the first floor of his house. He had a chair there too in the exercise room on the Strand level. He could get a closer look at her. She'd never see him through the tinted glass with the glare of the afternoon sun on it.

What he wanted was for something to push her over the edge, to make her angry enough to turn on the old man, to rail at him for his weakness, his distraction, his dependence on her, his inability to get better. Jack wouldn't be able to hear her. Even if she shouted, the wind would snatch the angry words away, but he didn't need to hear the words. He needed to see her snap. The old guy wasn't getting better. Her patience was clearly wasted on him.

Inevitably, though, she got the old man going again. Something she said made him turn his head into the wind toward the ocean. He stood and let the breeze buffet him as if he could take the wind into himself. For a moment the old man reminded Jack of the dog at his side. At times when they were out together, Soldier assumed that same posture of alert wariness, of sensing danger or possibility from the air itself. Jack's life depended on it.

The breeze brought a smile to the old man's face and pushed tears from his eyes. He turned to the woman, and they moved on. Tomorrow, Jack would spend the afternoon downstairs. Again, Soldier stirred under his hand. It was time for another round of Jack's therapy. He was not yet thirty, and he'd spent the last year working with doctors and sitting in specially built chairs. If he'd made any recovery, he couldn't see it. He'd be no match for the old guy in a race up the Strand, and if he didn't want to be led about for the rest of his life by some nursemaid, he had to get better.

***

When they were moving again, Mari glanced over her shoulder at the house that always stopped her grandpa in his tracks. A tall box of cement, glass, and steel—the place was totally out of character among the oversize shingled cottages mixed with Spanish contemporaries and the odd Tuscan villa or two lining the Strand. These were the houses of movers and shakers, people who'd made it big, or relatively big, in LA and who could now afford ocean-view real estate west of the Coast Highway.

While some homeowners clearly had more money than taste, most of them chose houses that looked cheerful and friendly: houses with little patios that opened to the Strand, lined with colorful planter boxes, with beach towels draped over the railings, and bikes or surfboards leaning up against weathered walls—houses that invited their occupants to get sun on their faces and sand between their toes.

For Mari, a walk on the Strand was like a tall drink of fresh-squeezed happy juice. The Strand was the un-freeway of LA. People walked dogs, moms pushed strollers, and surfers trotted across her path with wet tangled hair dripping on their shoulders, peeled-off black wet suits dangling from their waists to their knees, and sand clinging to their feet. Everybody said hi. The sun, or the fog when it was in, and the ocean and the wind did magic things to the senses. Today was no different. Even in November, the temperature was close to seventy, the sky was blue, and beachgoers had spread towels on the sand.

Her only problem with the Strand was the cement house. She knew her grandfather reacted as much to images from the past lurking on the dark memory paths of his brain as he did to the sensory details of the present. Once again, the glass and steel house set him off. It loomed dark and foreboding like something out of a Cold War spy movie. Part of her wanted to knock on the door or ring the bell and offer to put some big colorful planter pots on the sterile patio. A tub of pink geraniums, a yellow coreopsis or two, and some purple statice would make the place look less like a prison.

Recently, a series of small strokes had taken most of her grandfather's speech, so she couldn't ask him which memory the house triggered that agitated him, stopped him in his tracks, and caused him to shake. Once she pried his hands, with their surprisingly strong grip, from the lip of the thick glass barrier around the stark patio and turned his face back to the sea, he recovered.

Today, he had repeated the pattern, only a bit more strongly than usual, and he couldn't tell her what troubled him because his most recent stroke had reduced his speech to short outbursts. But they were in motion again, moving north, leaning into the wind, the fortress house with its steel and concrete, and the cold glitter of its windows like empty eyes, behind them.

She owed her knowledge of the Strand to her grandpa. He'd always required a close connection to the sea. The summer she turned seven, he and her grandmother Bernice had done the unthinkable for couples in their world at that time—they'd divorced. Her grandpa had moved out of the 1930s bungalow house on Tenth Street in San Pedro to the north side of the Palos Verdes hills. At the time it had seemed as if he'd gone to the other side of the moon. He'd purchased a sailboat to live on in a marina in Redondo Beach, and for three years, he simply disappeared.

Over three years later, her own dad finally visited his parent on his boat in the marina. Mari had begged to go along, and she'd kept going on her own by bus whenever she could. A visit with Grandpa Connor in her eleventh summer meant a sail on his boat, a fish or two to clean, and a bike ride on the Strand to their favorite burrito stand. She'd studied her grandpa closely on those visits, weighing what she heard on her family's side of the hill with what she saw for herself. Those visits had made her a different person from her two older brothers and older sister, who sided with her grandmother. The summer her father first took her to see Grandpa was the summer Mari had learned to look for the other side to every story.

People from their old neighborhood considered themselves real people, the salt of the earth with real jobs. They operated cranes, piloted boats, kept machines running, and made sure goods made it in and out of LA Harbor. In their view, people on the LA side of the hill had phony jobs, played at life, tossed volleyballs around on the beach, or starred in movies. She regularly had to shrug off family and friends' comments about her fluff job as community relations director for the small, upscale Coast Plaza Mall.

But one of the perks of the job had been reconnecting with Grandpa Connor after years of not seeing him much. He'd never been around at Christmas in Mari's teenage or college years, especially after Grandma Bernice had taken up with her second husband Ron. But ever since Mari's first year at Coast Plaza, she had seen him often. Grandpa Connor had become a favorite Santa's Workshop Santa. His smiling face wreathed in a white beard appeared in eight-by-ten glossies next to the faces of hundreds of little boys and girls.

Last Christmas she'd seen him almost every day. That was before his strokes. Now her cousin Abby, a trained nurse, had temporarily taken over as Grandpa Connor's caregiver at the Redondo Beach house he'd purchased when he'd sold the sailboat. Abby had definite ideas about what was best for him. Any sign a walk had upset him or made him difficult to manage later in the evening was fuel for Abby's argument about what to do with Grandpa. And selling Grandpa's house was the best way to afford the 24/7 care Abby believed he needed. Abby, like most of the family, couldn't think of Grandpa Connor's house without seeing dollar signs.

In spite of the cement house on the Strand, Mari had no intention of giving up her outings with her grandpa. She could tell him anything. Even now, after his strokes, she kept up a cheerful monologue about the family and herself. Today she told him how she'd started dating again. It was time. Her brief experiment in unengaged cohabitation had ended nearly a year ago. She'd been conned by one of the oldest ruses around. Grant had suggested they live together while he finished his MBA. It was never said, but always implied, when he got his degree their real life together would begin. It'd been wrenching to realize as his graduation approached that she'd been a convenience more than a girlfriend, and that there was no future for them. Moving out had taken all her resolve and most of her savings, but she was back on her own two feet. The trick now would be not to let herself be misled again.

When she and Grandpa Connor reached their turnaround point, Mari squeezed his hand and waited for an answering squeeze. It came, and for a moment he seemed to know her, his eyes clear and smiling with the old playfulness that'd made him game for anything on her summer visits to his boat in the old days.

The happy look faded, and he stumbled a bit. She steadied him as they turned and headed south, the wind at their backs to blow them all the way home. She was sure she would know the shape and feel of her grandfather's hand if all her other senses went away.

***

Jack's therapy session ended, as the sessions often did, with his body spasming with dry heaves. That was the goal—to push himself to the point of dizziness and to tolerate more and more punishment along the way. He could almost do all of the movements without losing his balance. But they were exercises in a controlled environment done under the supervision of his trainer. He was impatient to test himself in the real world. He'd been asking Cole about it for weeks.

Jack leaned back against the upright, padded bench of the cage breathing carefully, bringing the nausea under control. Cole handed him a towel, and he pressed it to his face. He'd chosen Cole Walker as a trainer because the guy was tough. He made their sessions as punishing and unforgiving as only a true disciple of the "no-pain-no-gain" school of thought could. Cole had set up the house's ground level workout room with Jack and the team in mind, but the cage was Jack's go-to machine. It looked something like a Transformer toy from Jack's childhood with its arms and pulleys and adjustable back pad, and it allowed Jack to exercise different muscle groups from a seated position without moving his head.

Controlling his head movements had been the key from the moment his doctors had identified the injury to his balance system. It had a name and an acronym that began with the word "benign." As far as Jack was concerned, there was nothing benign about the loose bits of crystal floating in his inner ear that messed with his balance.

"You're ready, man. You've got to get out there. No wimping out."

Instinctively, Jack started to reach for Soldier and stopped himself. Soldier was off duty, outside having a romp in a local park with Rashaad, burning off doggie energy so he'd be ready to return to Jack's side later.

"Ready for what?" He kept the towel pressed to his face. The nausea started to recede.

Cole returned weights to the rack, careful not to let the bars ring against the metal rod, a noise that could trigger Jack's dizziness. "Pushing a shopping cart through your local supermarket would be a good test."

He wanted to laugh, but another spasm threatened. So that's where all the hard work led. Cole considered him ready to drive a shopping cart. It might be a big advance from where he'd been, but it wasn't exactly the nimble maneuverability of an action hero. So much for Jack's fantasies of taking on the world. The pathetic thing was, to Jack, pushing a shopping cart sounded like a nightmare.

"Come on, Ryker. You in, or are you my 'wimp of the week?'" Jack must've done well today, because for Cole the insult was mild. "Tomorrow we'll do a session at the supermarket. Get your people to deliver you there at five."

After Cole left, Jack returned to the chair at his upstairs window where Soldier, back from the park, lay at his feet. It would be an hour or more before Jack felt like eating. The sun was down, the sky still aglow with golds and purples. He wouldn't see the woman again today, but the temptation to find out who she was lingered. He should let it go. He'd had no woman in his life for years, and he had no business trying to meet a woman now. It'd been nearly six months since his enemy's last attempt on his life, but Frank Evans was still out there, still a threat.

Jack waited until the sky went black before he gave in to temptation and called Marcus, his head of security, to review the tapes. He gave the day, time, and camera number. When asked what he was looking for, he explained an old guy had grabbed the glass panel around the patio. His security team would take that kind of activity seriously.

When his phone buzzed a few minutes later, he opened a picture with the woman and the old man in the frame. Marcus was apologetic.

"We shouldn't have missed this, Ryker. It might be easier to track down the woman first with social media. Then we'll get the old guy. Give us a few minutes."

"No worries. Getting her is good too." Soldier nudged his knee, but Jack kept his hand on his phone. He thought he'd been casual enough, giving away nothing of his interest, letting Marcus think Jack merely wanted him to check a security matter.

Streetlamps illuminated the Strand at night, and the sky above LA was never wholly dark, so Jack sat far enough back from the window to remain in the shadows. He was never dizzy in the dark: the blacker, the better. Nothing confused his senses in the dark. He could concentrate on the alignment of his limbs in perfect symmetry. He felt balanced.

His phone buzzed again a short while later. His guys were good, the best. They'd learned security in a hard school.

"Okay, Ryker. The old guy is Connor Lynch, eighty-five, retired harbor pilot." Jack listened carefully. He'd trained his people to speak slowly and not put too much information into their brief reports, but tonight his head of security went on a bit about Lynch's work history, his financials, and his origins. "He worked a fishing boat with his sons for almost fifteen years, has a house in Redondo Beach, an ex-wife in San Pedro, and he had a stroke last January. In the nineties, he spent three years in a Sinaloa prison." Jack waited, trying not to let the fire hose of info set off an episode of dizziness. "You ready for this? The old guy's been playing Santa Claus at the local mall for the last three years." Marcus paused.

"And the woman?" Jack kept his voice neutral.

"The woman is Maryrose Lynch, Connor's granddaughter. Twenty-eight, went to Mary Star of the Sea in San Pedro, and Boston College. She goes by Mari on social media. She's community relations director for the Coast Plaza Mall, has the back unit of a house on Ninth. No roommate, no pets. She's squeaky clean, a real girl scout. Good credit scores. No criminal record. No traffic violations. Parents alive, living in Pedro. Two older brothers. One older sister."

Jack asked Marcus to save the data and dismissed him with a slight movement of his left hand. Tomorrow he would examine the file and make a plan to meet the maddeningly kind and patient Maryrose Lynch.

Chapter 2

Mari sat at one of the round tables dotting the mall's "community" room, in the corner reserved for her Santa interviews. She faced her seventh Santa of the afternoon, her last. He was another white Santa. She hadn't had any responses yet to her postings for a Black Santa.

This candidate, like all prospective Santas, had been fingerprinted and background checked before he reached the interview stage. She had read close to fifty resumes and studied headshots and references from Santa agencies like the Kringle Group. The Coast Plaza preferred local retirees for Santa work. This Santa had played a bit of minor league baseball in his youth, done a lot of residential construction work, and now had arthritis, and he confessed his wife wanted him out of the house for a while. He was bald, but he had a white mustache and the requisite jolly face, and he belonged to a local amateur theater group.

So far, Mari hadn't found the right Santa to replace Grandpa on Saturdays. A Saturday Santa had to be the most resilient, kid-friendly, unflappable sort of Santa, one who could handle the all-day stream of families. She'd seen some pretty jaded Santas so far. She had high hopes for this one. He looked good in the Santa suit. Now if he could pass the "hot seat" test of a few challenging scenarios and the heat in the community room, he would go to the top of her list of callbacks.

When they finished the preliminaries, Mari handed him the final Santa props—hat and wig, wire-rimmed glasses, and white gloves—and sat him in the green velvet Santa chair with a large doll and the mall "Santa" script, a group of lines Santa needed to be comfortable saying. They would do a bit of role-playing, so Mari could judge this Santa's ability to calm a frightened child or keep an overly demanding one in check. And she wanted to hear his Santa laugh to judge how genuine a *Ho ho ho* he could manage. Finally, she would ask him how he felt about the inevitable downsides of playing Santa for six hours at a stretch in a chair, under lights in a suit that could get hot and itchy. The kids on Santa's lap might be dressed up to have their pictures taken, but they were still little kids. Some were going to cough, sneeze, cry, pee, or even puke on Santa. Some would challenge him and pull his glasses or his beard. And the kids' parents could be a big negative in the equation too. Standing in long lines for a photo-op never improved anyone's temperament.

She smiled at the Santa candidate. "Ready?"

"Ho, ho, ho. Merry Christmas. What's your name?"

"Tracy." She gave herself the cool, contemporary name she'd wanted in kindergarten.

"Have you been a good girl this year, Tracy?" Santa focused his attention on the doll in his lap, a good sign that he understood his role.

Mari nodded solemnly, channeling her inner five-year-old self.

"What do you want most for Christmas?"

"A puppy." She was throwing him a curveball, but she needed to see how he'd react.

"A puppy? What kind of puppy?"

Okay, he hadn't panicked, and he hadn't shut the little girl's wish down, but the line was long. He couldn't get off track. Mari pushed a little harder. "The kind Kendra has."

"Who's Kendra?"

Oops. She could hear a note of dismay in Santa's voice, he was getting off track, and he had a long line of people waiting for him. Mari pushed him again. "Kendra's my friend. Her mom and dad gave her a puppy."

"Ah," said Santa. "Ho ho ho. I'm glad you told me that, Tracy." He bounced the doll on his knee. "I see that you understand where puppies come from—from moms and dads. Is there something you think *Santa* could bring you, from my *toy* shop?"

Mari smiled. *Nice recovery, Santa.* She gave him points for remembering the little girl's name, for bringing the conversation back to toys, and for not promising a puppy. This Santa could be the one. She hoped he could tolerate the heat of the lighted Santa's workshop and the long hours in the chair with little opportunity to stretch his limbs. She had him read some more of Santa's most famous lines while she flipped through her script, looking for a challenging boy scenario. To train its Santas, the mall had collected tough kid responses over the years. One of the hardest ones for all Santas to deflect was the charge that they weren't real. And, of course, they weren't.

Her phone buzzed, and Mari gave it a quick glance. The date she planned to meet in fifteen minutes at the coffee bar at the far end of the mall had sent her a text.

Something came up. Catch you later.

No apology. No regret. Just like that she felt the air go out of her happy balloon. She looked at Santa and tried to recover her enthusiasm for him, but now he looked too tired for the job.

Mari reminded herself that it wasn't his fault that dating during the holidays sucked. She and her friend Shanny could name ten cute movies in which strangers instantly connected and a montage or two later ended up decorating a tree together and pledging undying love. The genre had permanently skewed female expectations, and Mari imagined a warning label to accompany such films.

It is known to the State of California that watching romantic Christmas movies raises harmful expectations in the female breast. Watch responsibly.

She turned her phone over on the table and picked up a boy doll for Santa for their next role play. Santa settled the boy doll on his knee and nodded at her.

"Ho, ho, ho, what's your name, son?" Santa began.

"I'm not your son. My dad's a pilot." Mari imagined a skinny six-year-old with his arms folded across his chest. The boy probably felt silly sitting on Santa's lap.

"What does your dad fly?" Santa asked.

"He flies the 737-700."

"That's a big plane, much bigger than my sleigh. Ho, ho, ho."

"You don't really fly, do you? You're just a big fat…fake." As Mari said it, she understood the fictional little boy she'd created. The adults in his life had disappointed him, made him distrustful and suspicious of goodness.

"You know why I'm fat, don't you?"

Mari paused. Santa number seven had some good instincts, but a sheen of sweat gleamed on his brow.

"My dad's not fat." She felt mean keeping the pressure on.

Santa shifted in his chair. He held the boy doll lightly. "What do you want your dad to bring you for Christmas?"

"He should come home. He should stop chasing that woman around and come home."

Santa gave the doll a slight squeeze on the shoulder. "I'll put that on your list. One dad home for Christmas."

"You can't do that. You don't even know me. I never said my name."

"Santa has his ways. Do you want a picture with Santa?"

Mari shook her head. Of course, it wasn't the boy's choice. There would be a mom or a grandmother making that decision. If that adult had not already been appalled by the boy's "too much information" dump. It happened. It was not uncommon in fact for kids to reveal to Santa, and everyone else in line, just what was going on in their families financially and emotionally.

She nodded to Santa seven and made some notes on her clipboard. He had some real Santa potential. He stood up, straightened his back, and sighed. "Phew. Is that what Santa gets from these kids?"

"It's a taste. I gave you a couple of the hard ones, but the harder thing is how many there are and how different and yet the same each kid is. The job requires a lot of patience and…empathy."

Santa loosened his fur-lined collar. His face had reddened considerably during the session.

Mari glanced at her phone again. No messages. She remembered that she didn't have to be anywhere. She handed Santa a card with the mall's HR number and email address. "Thank you for coming in today. We should know our staffing needs soon and be in touch with you by next week." She directed him back to the curtained alcove where he could return to his street clothes, and as he passed her, she got a whiff of Santa sweat, a sour, pungent odor like gym socks.

Mari made a note on her clipboard. Either Santa would need a new deodorant, or some child was going to announce, "Santa, you stink" to the whole mall.

***

Jack's driver parked the black SUV in a handicapped spot in front of the supermarket at the south end of the Coast Plaza Mall's vast parking lot. He told Soldier to stay and climbed out of the vehicle.

While his crew fanned out and did a quick sweep of the parking lot and supermarket, he steadied himself. He stood alone, no dog, no cane, no walking sticks in a public place with ordinary people for the first time in two years.

He knew he didn't look out of place. He'd dressed the part of a young South Bay professional—a dark plaid, collared shirt from the surf shop on the Avenue, hung over his khakis. His longish hair met his shirt collar and concealed the tattoos, both the ones his captors had given him and the ones he'd had added to disguise their handiwork. His dark glasses and flip-flops completed the look. No one would glance at him twice.

The automatic doors opened and closed behind entering customers, people intent on their errands, hardly noticing their surroundings. To his right in one of two chains of shopping carts, the final skewed cart was jammed in such a way that no one could pull it free. He'd have to go for a cart from the other chain.

The black box secure communication device at his waist buzzed. There was apparently no sign of a threat. The test was a go. Cole was in the market, ready to track his progress and offer obstacles. Jack had known Cole would make it challenging, and he had fifteen minutes to get fifteen items from ten aisles and make it to the express check-out stand.

He pivoted carefully, keeping his gaze focused on the cart chain. *Spotting*. It was a trick that dancers used to make their endless turns. No dizziness. His hands met the cart handle, and he pulled until the thing slid free of its fellows. He backed up a couple steps and swung the front of the cart around, keeping his head steady, letting his eyes follow the motion, then pointed his cart toward the doors. They opened, and he pushed in.

So far, so good.

Eggs. Item one on Cole's list.

The clock was ticking, but he took a minute to orient himself. Cole probably assumed that Jack knew his way around a grocery store, but he'd never spent much time in supermarkets. His parents had had an efficient staff to do the shopping, cooking, cleaning, gardening, and much more. Once in a while, Paloma, his nanny, had taken him with her to pick up some forgotten item. He'd been small enough then to ride in the cart.

Now he scanned the layout, looking for signage to direct him. He didn't need to look at Cole's list. At least that part of his brain still worked. He could glance at a printed page and remember its contents. He held his head still and let his gaze sweep the store to his left. Bright pots of wine-colored plants in the floral department smelled earthy and herby. People queued up at a glassed-in area marked by a black mortar and pestle with the Rx character on the pestle. Ahead of him an open area of raised produce bins displayed mounds of yams and potatoes, and beyond them avocados, brussels sprouts, and onions. Beyond the bins of vegetables, tall glass-doored dairy cases lined the back wall of the store. He shoved the cart forward.

***

Mari slipped a plastic basket over her arm at the supermarket entrance, still thinking about her Santa problem. Even if the last candidate worked out, she needed at least two more Santas, and one of them had to be a replacement for her previous Black Santa. She had put out some calls and posted the job on the mall's website, but had yet to hear back from anyone. A frown from a woman trying to maneuver a cart past Mari in the narrow space between pots of burgundy chrysanthemums and the stacks of turkey stuffing boxes brought her back to the present.

Mari stepped aside, murmuring an "excuse me" to the woman, and tried to focus on her errand. With her cancelled date, she needed to think about dinner. It wouldn't simply hop into her basket. She headed for the eggs, pretty sure she was out of them. The relentless upbeat piped-in music shifted from one pop version of a standard holiday song to another. She had a random thought that the watered-down tunes had lost their power to move the spirit like the ancient, minor-key church songs of her childhood.

When she reached it, the egg case had been thoroughly picked over. She leaned in to look at what was left, her mom's lessons in frugality at war with a desire to support local farms, as local as farms could be in sprawling LA. In the far bottom corner of the case, she spotted a container of brown, cage-free eggs, hand-stamped with the logo of a farm in the west San Fernando Valley.

As she lifted her prize, then turned away—the end of another shopper's cart collided with her hand and sent the eggs flying. They landed on the linoleum with a container-crushing splat. Her knuckles stung from the sharp blow, and her gaze swung round to the driver of the cart.

He was tall and broad-shouldered, with collar-length dark hair, loose around a chiseled face, and eyes hidden behind military-style dark glasses. His hands had a death grip on the cart handle, and he was breathtaking, in a frozen sort of way. She couldn't decide whether he had entered some hyperalert state or was utterly aloof, somewhere inside himself away from the buzz of the shifting crowd around them, the flickering glare of the fluorescent lights, and the jingling noise of the holiday pop medley. His gaze focused on her hand, and she lifted it to show him that it was okay. The front edge of his cart had opened a thin red gash across the tops of her fingers, and she shook her hand.

Because he seemed incapable of speech, she spoke. "I'm okay, really," she assured him.

"Your eggs." She thought his hidden gaze shifted to the broken carton on the floor.

"Replaceable." His head didn't move. She suspected he was memorizing the carton.

"You picked those eggs." He seemed unaware that he was staring, holding up his fellow shoppers and failing to apologize. People around them cast annoyed looks their way and shoved their carts around the egg mess on the floor.

Mari should call him on his rudeness, snap him out of whatever trance he had fallen into, but she fell into a trance of her own, willing to go on looking at him a while longer. Really, men like him didn't show up on her dating app.

"Just eggs," she said, stepping back and breaking the spell. "I'll get management to clean up the mess and pick another carton. It's all good. We're good."

She sensed his eyes behind the dark lenses following her little move. "Maryrose Lynch." His voice was a low, rough-edged whisper full of wonder.

"What?" She put her hand to her jacket lapel as if she'd find a name badge there. No badge.

A large man appeared at her side, crowding her so that she instinctively shifted to one side. "Can I help you, miss?" he asked.

Mari turned to tell him she was fine and stopped. In a black knit pullover shirt with an earbud in one ear and a thin wire snaking down his thick neck, the man was no store employee. He had wandered in from a movie set of some espionage thriller. Beyond his bulk, a blond teenager in the store's red-shirt-and-black-slacks uniform efficiently swept the egg debris into a dustpan and wiped the floor with a rag.

Mari squared her shoulders and looked straight up into the large man's grim, expressionless face. A cinder block had more distinguishing features. He was looking at her, but she suspected he was listening to a message in his ear.

"No thank you," she told him, "Just give me some space, and I'll get on with my shopping."

Mr. Super-Sized moved slightly, blocking Mari's view of the beautiful stranger who had spoken her name. She turned to the empty shelves of the egg case, trying to concentrate. Super-Sized still loomed over her left shoulder. She reached for an egg carton, keeping her hand steady. She was just a woman doing an errand in a friendly grocery store, no need to imagine a spy-thriller scenario about to go down. Without lifting her head, she glanced up at the security mirror attached to the wall, high up in the corner.

Reflected in its gleaming round surface was the plaid back of the stranger as he pushed his cart down the toiletries aisle, an ordinary shopper, picking up a few items on the way home from work. Except he hadn't been ordinary, and there was nothing ordinary about the matching pair of large men in black shirts moving in perfect parallel with him along the flanking aisles of the market.

Chapter 3

At seven, Mari took her laptop out onto the small deck of her apartment. Her second-story unit at the back of a walk street cottage overlooking an alley gave her a view of her neighbors' cars and trash bins. On the other hand, she could see sky, smell the ocean, and hear waves breaking, and she settled into her padded wicker chair. She was expecting a knock from her landlady, who was about to take off for three weeks of visiting her grandchildren in Oregon.

Usually, sky and waves were enough to settle Mari's mind, but tonight she kept thinking back to the incident in the grocery store. It was weird enough that the stranger had—what?—his own security detail, and a supersized one at that? But it was weirder still that he knew her name, her full real name, and that he'd spoken it as if the name itself were a wonder, a name she had been eager to shed in childhood as uncool and old-fashioned. He must have looked at some online source, maybe more than one, maybe even her dating profile, but he hadn't expected to meet her. Their meeting had been accidental, and apparently, his bodyguards hadn't liked it.

But she had no time for beautiful strangers or no-show dates. With her computer on her lap desk, she opened the Santa Candidates folder in her work email. Her top priority was to find a Saturday Santa in time to rehearse Santa's Friday-after-Thanksgiving arrival at the mall. She clicked open an attachment from a new candidate. He had included a picture of himself in flowered Hawaiian shirt over red board shorts, dark glasses perched on his Santa hat, a toy sack over his shoulder, and a surfboard under his arm. It was a cute concept, but he looked twenty-four, tops. Mari moved on. She didn't need the historical St. Nicholas, Turkish bishop and patron saint of sailors and maidens, but she wasn't ready for "Surfin' Santa."

She scrolled to another email from a little community center off the Coast Highway, a place that she often passed on her way to visit her family. The youth programs director wrote that they might have a Black Santa for her, and she started to read about the possible Santa when her phone pinged with a text.

Cousin Abby.

What did you do to Grandpa yesterday?

Mari texted back a *hello*, replied that they had done their usual walk, and made a mental note to change their Strand route to avoid the cement house. She didn't want to cause Grandpa trouble with Abby. Faint dots danced in the text bubble on her phone as Abby typed a reply.

A sharp rap sounded on her door, and she set her laptop aside and headed downstairs as the insistent knock came again.

When she opened the door, she came face-to-face not with her kindly landlady but with the supersize man from the supermarket, Cinder Block, in his black shirt with the neck wire snaking from his ear to his collar.

"Ms. Lynch," he said. "Your eggs." He held out a clear plastic bag with a carton of the brand of local cage-free eggs she'd dropped in the market. "Sorry for the inconvenience earlier."

Mari stared at the bag dangling from his huge hand. The moment in the grocery store came back to her, the intensity of the stranger's gaze on her and then on her eggs. A thought flashed in her head like a warning light on her car dash.

"He knows where I live?" *Mistake.* It made no sense to show nervousness to large, strange men at your door. She should say thank you, take the bag, and close the door, but the words didn't come.

Cinder Block, his mouth a grim line, lowered the bag to her doorstep. "There you go, miss."

He backed away. Footsteps coming along the walk from the front of the house distracted her. Cinder Block had reached the alley before she shouted, "Wait. He knows where I live?" No answer. No sound. She dashed for the alley and looked up its length. *Where could a man that big get to that fast?* She didn't see him, only shadows and dark places, hiding places behind cars or the corners of buildings. Cinder Block hadn't triggered any of her neighbors' motion lights. He'd just vanished. She listened for a car, but only the Number 30 bus rumbled by on the avenue at the upper end of the alley.

"Mari?" her landlady called from in front of Mari's door.

Mari turned back. “Sorry, Vera. I…just had a delivery, didn’t get to tip the guy. You have keys for me?”

“Yes.” Her landlady began to explain the plant watering routine she wanted Mari to follow in her absence.

Mari’s phone pinged again, and she glanced at Abby’s text. It was long and angry, but very, very clear.

I’m not letting Grandpa walk with you anymore.

***

Jack was back in his chair, Soldier alert at his side. He’d made the dog uneasy. With his chin, Soldier nudged Jack’s elbow to release his grip on the chair arm. No one on Jack’s team said a word about the fiasco at the grocery store. They had cleaned up his mess and kept him safe. That’s what they were paid to do, but it was what they did for other reasons too, reasons that stretched back to the far-flung reaches of mountainous Taliban territory where US Marines tried to win ground for Afghan security forces and where a group of them had paid a high price to rescue Jack, a civilian, from his captors. Marine by marine, Jack was repaying them for that sacrifice.

Discipline—that was the distinguishing trait of a marine. Jack thought he’d achieved a measure of that discipline and earned his team’s respect until he’d come face-to-face with Maryrose Lynch in a grocery store. Seeing her so near made him forget the plan, forget Cole’s drill, forget everything he’d come to LA to do.

She was all that his enemy, the object of their mission, was not. Her face was open, nothing hidden in the deep espresso-colored eyes. She had serious straight dark brows, the wide mouth made for laughing, and a stubborn pointed chin in an almost square jaw. She had stared at him as frankly as he had stared at her. Then he’d seen the scratch across her knuckles, and like an idiot, he had spoken her name.

He wanted to see her again with a consuming impatience that had to be controlled. He needed a plan. He knew from the brief profile his team had already collected on her that Maryrose was dating, using an app to meet men. It would be easy for his guys to set up a phony profile matched to the kind of man she was likely to go for, but he wanted no electronic trail connecting her to him. He had created his own SCIF on the Strand, what the intelligence community in DC called a "sensitive compartmentalized information facility." Nothing in or out, and that had to be the rule until he and the team finished the mission.

A more direct approach would be to have his security guys stop her as she walked past Jack's house with her grandfather, but he didn't see that as a winning strategy, either. The more he thought about it, the more he saw that arranging to meet Maryrose was not a task for his team. He needed a different sort of help with this one, and he did need help. He could admit that. His old enemies from his Canyon School days, Sloan and Huntington, who had not truly been his enemies, and whom he could now count as friends, if he had friends, would know what to do. Huntington had been capable of seducing almost any woman in his path, and even Sloan, who had only ever had eyes for one woman, knew a thing or two about them. Jack knew nothing.

He got a text from security. *Eggs delivered.*

He loosened his grip on the chair and let his hand rest on Soldier's silky head. Tomorrow Jack would call Huntington. If anyone knew how to meet a girl without screwing up, Huntington knew.

***

Josh Huntington had his hands in a sink full of dish water in his apartment's tiny open kitchen when the call came. Emma, his love and bride-to-be, folded laundry behind him on the table in their living room, and Max, her six-year-old, sat in his bedroom doing homework. A promise had been made of hot chocolate and stories when the work was done. Josh and Max liked to compete to see how many mini marshmallows each of them could float in the top of a mug of hot cocoa.

"Emma." He still called her Emma, even now when he knew her birth name. "That could be the woman from the mall about a Santa." Emma crossed the open room, fished his buzzing phone out of his back pocket, and showed him the number while he dried his hands.

He nodded and took the phone from her, thumb swiping to answer the call. She gave him a kiss on the cheek. The silence at the other end tempted Josh to disconnect, but he hung on for a few more beats, watching Emma turn toward the hall to her son's bedroom. It wasn't the woman from the mall, but Jack Ryker. It was the first time Ryker had called Josh directly. Usually, he heard from one of the large capable individuals Ryker called his "team."

Josh listened, slightly astonished at the unexpected request. It was a short call. Ryker wasn't one for chewing the fat. Josh offered to help and hoped he betrayed none of the amusement he felt at the irony of the situation. He and Ryker and Sloan remained bound together by a single incident in the last days of their senior year at Canyon Prep Boys School and their mutual contempt for Canyon's corrupt, and now disgraced, former Head of School. Together the three of them had engineered the head's downfall and the survival of the school.

When Emma returned, Josh was staring out the apartment window, thinking about how to help Ryker as a fog bank gathered on the horizon. Emma slid her arms around Josh's waist and waited for him to speak.

"Jack Ryker wants to meet a woman," he said. "Not just any woman. He's picked one out, apparently."

"He's your friend from the Grindstone concert? The one with the black lab dog that took care of Max?" Emma slipped to Josh's side without breaking contact.

"Yes. 'Friend' might be a slight overstatement."

"So, naturally, he called an expert on women, you." She nudged Josh in the ribs.

He kissed the top of her head. "An expert who specializes in one woman." Josh meant to get a PhD in Emma studies. They would be married with much fanfare in the spring from her grandparents' house, a concession to parental sensibilities on both sides. So far, he had resisted other parental pressure, to take a job in the financial sector, to go back to receiving his trust. It meant staying in their apartment and postponing a part of Emma's promise to Max that they get a dog. He was still working on that one.

"What sage advice did you offer him?" Emma asked.

"It's tricky," Josh said. "Hard to know what's going on behind those dark glasses, and I think he has a balance problem."

"Oh," said Emma, "that chair of his. It's not a wheelchair, is it?"

"No." Josh had a clear memory of a photo of Ryker surrounded by arms-buying heavies at IDEX, the International Defense Exhibition and Conference in Abu Dhabi in 2011. "Before he returned to LA, he was in the habit of frequenting places the State Department warns Americans to avoid. He didn't get those neck tattoos in Venice Beach, and I'm guessing he was already the walking wounded when we knew him at Canyon because of something Headmaster Chambers did to him."

"The headmaster damaged him?"

"Not literally. But Chambers made Ryker angry enough to burn down the school sign and skip graduation."

"Wow. That is angry. Wasn't Ryker the brains of your class?"

"Other than Sloan, yes."

"So, what does he do now?"

Josh turned Emma in his arms to give her another kiss. "He inherited a fortune and acres of California real estate, and runs a foundation that supports wounded veterans. And he hires massive security guys. I gather someone tried to kill him at the Grindstone concert in May. I don't think he's resolved all his anger issues."

"Did he say who the woman he wants to meet is?"

Josh shook his head. "Not yet. I told him to have the dog with him if he could."

"Very wise," said Emma. She pulled out of his hold. "You've earned your cocoa and marshmallows."

***

Mari headed for the Strand a little after five. Bands of red and purple clouds marked the horizon where the sun had dropped into the sea. At work she'd finally connected with Josh Huntington, the community center youth programs director, who gave her a lead on a Black Santa. She pulled her hair into a ponytail and secured it with a scrunchie from her vest pocket. Without Grandpa Connor, she was going for a run. Abby said he was doing better. Mari doubted it. She believed he needed those walks by the sea. But she had to admit that she'd made a mistake taking him by the cement house.

As she approached it, she slowed her run to check the place out. The three-story rectangular block of a house took up a double lot on the north side of a walk street running uphill from the Strand. Rough horizontal ridges from the concrete forms made bands on the gray walls. Two upper decks and a lower patio had floor-to-ceiling tinted windows facing the sea. The other windows were mere vertical slits in the side of the house. There was no visible door. The grim aesthetic was a cross between parking structure and fortress. Mari thought the place could repel Attila the Hun should he come calling. The puzzle of her grandpa's reaction to it remained.

For curiosity's sake, she turned up the walk street. A tall, spiked, iron railing enclosed a stone path along the side of the house, and a windowless square cement tower at the rear rose the height of the building. As Mari pondered what the tower might house, the distinctive whiff of cigarette smoke reached her. She took a few steps and peered around the edge of the tower. A man leaned against a door at its base.

She recognized the smoking man at once. He was Cinder Block in his black shirt with his earbud and wire. He drew in another drag, put out the lit end between his fingertips, and dropped the butt in a pocket. Then he saw her. He mouthed something, but she didn't hear what he said. A car alarm went off somewhere nearby. He tried to smile, but she didn't think his facial muscles knew how.

"Hello," she called, stepping up to the iron railing. "He's in there, isn't he? I want to see him." She knew who lived there as soon as she saw Cinder Block, and she realized that the whole point of the fortress-like house was to prevent anyone from seeing him, the beautiful stranger from the supermarket.

Cinder Block cupped his mouth with one hand and turned aside to speak to someone on the other end of his wire. As the car alarm stopped, Cinder Block turned back to her, something clicked, and a gate in the iron railing swung open. Mari stepped inside.

"Ms. Lynch, he'll see you now. Please leave your phone with me."

Mari didn't say any of the rude things she was thinking as Cinder Block extended a large hand for her phone. "Nothing here is illegal. You are in no danger."

No, she thought, *your boss is in danger of having me tell him what I think.* Mari handed over her phone. Cinder Block turned it off and slipped it into a padded metallic bag, then stepped aside and gestured to the path. At the door to the tower, he halted, tipped his face up, and waited. Mari followed his glance, expecting a security camera, and saw nothing. Plenty of pricey beach houses had those little octagonal signs on the property warning of twenty-four-hour surveillance or armed response, but Cinder Block was a whole new level of security. The door slid open. She had a fleeting thought that she was nuts to enter the place, but she remembered that she had a few things to say to the stranger. If he had done an Internet search on her because her grandpa held on to the glass partition at the front of his property, that was nutty, that was paranoia.

Inside was a small vestibule and a closed stainless-steel elevator door. They passed the elevator, and Cinder Block opened a door into a ground floor gym or a workout room. Mari hesitated while her eyes adjusted to the deeper gloom. Nothing scary met her gaze, only yoga mats on the floor, weights in their racks, and fitness machines for several different muscle groups.

"He'll see you now." Cinder Block indicated a man in a chair, facing the ocean, a large black Labrador retriever at his side.

Mari took a steadying breath and crossed the gym, ready to give him a piece of her mind. Then face-to-face with him again, she stopped dead, caught as she'd been in the grocery store by his appearance.

He'd been working out, apparently. His collar-length dark hair was damp, and she could plainly see the tattoos on his neck under the sheen of perspiration. A sweat-darkened charcoal gray T-shirt clung to his chest. His arms, very strong arms, rested on some sort of mechanized chair. The black chair puzzled her. It wasn't a wheelchair, and a pair of navy workout shorts revealed his perfectly healthy-looking legs and bare feet. She knew he could walk: He'd plowed into her in the supermarket.

"You got the eggs," he said. The dark glasses hid his eyes.

She nodded. "You know my name. You know where I live." Mari made the words an accusation, a challenge. He remained silent, and his silence gave her time to realize that he was steps ahead of her. He must have already figured out that she'd found him through Cinder Block.

"I'm Jack."

She wanted to say that the tiny exchange of personal information didn't make them even. She wanted to know who he really was and why the chair and the dark glasses and the dog and the beefy security men and the fortress.

"You didn't bring your grandfather today," he said.

"Is there anything you *don't* know about me?" She had thought her personal information fairly secure. Suddenly she imagined that everything she'd ever said or done had somehow been exposed to this man's gaze. Maybe paranoia was catching.

"Yes."

"That's meant to be comforting?" Mari waited for him to say more. She was kind of stuck on his beautiful mouth while her brain tried to make sense of the vast pauses between his terse comments. She was used to the quick back-and-forth of her large family, of people interrupting and speaking over one another.

"Is your grandfather okay?"

"He had a stroke recently. He's not himself anymore."

"My house bothers him."

"It does," she agreed. "I have no idea why. It's such a cheerful, warm, inviting sort of fortress." She couldn't keep a little sarcasm from creeping in. He'd seen her with Grandpa Connor. He'd seen them stop. There probably were cameras even if she hadn't spotted them. He held himself so still, his body aligned in perfect symmetry at odds with the asymmetry of the way he talked. She imagined her words wandering down long dark corridors in his brain before they reached headquarters and elicited a return message.

"You date," he said.

"Do you?" He could not have *dated* in the twenty-first century. If he thought dating was a thing people still did, he must have been trapped in his concrete fortress a long time.

"I want to date you."

"Date me?" Her voice squeaked. Her legs went rubbery, and she sat down. On the floor. The dog immediately lowered his belly to the floor to face her. She didn't know whether the man or the dog watched her more intently. Again, her brain worked to process what was going on inside his head. He was puzzling, and vulnerable, and he wanted to date her, the strangest, most beautiful man she'd ever not really met. No labor-intensive series of swipes to get matches to get a phone number to get to a date, just a bold assertion. He hadn't made the effort to find her name and her address because she and her grandpa had come too close to his house. He didn't regard her as some kind of security threat.

"What's your idea of a date?" she asked.

"My friend says..." he began.

"You have a friend?" She knew it was rude to sound so incredulous.

He held up two fingers.

"Oh, two. You're not counting the dog, are you?"

He lifted a third finger. She thought his mouth twitched. It was probably as close to a laugh as he could get.

"I interrupted you," she said. "You started to tell me your idea of a date."

"Dinner," he said.

"Dinner? Just you and me and your very own well-muscled secret service detail?" She wondered how many of them there were. "Do you simply take over a restaurant?"

"Here," he said. "To watch the sunset."

Five words strung together. He was waxing eloquent, making a romantic suggestion, and he'd thought about it. He already had a plan. She wished she could see his eyes, could understand the contradictions in front of her—the chair that held him motionless in his workout room, the hiddenness of his eyes and frankness of his words, the slowness of his speech and quickness of his mind.

"Do you eat?" he asked.

She laughed. He'd made a joke. Humor was high on her list of date requirements. "I'm trying to understand this. You. You saw me walking on the Strand with my grandpa, so you decided to ask me out?"

"You don't lose patience with him."

The quickness of the reply stopped her thoughts. Mari held herself still, trying not to reveal by so much as a flicker of her gaze how unguarded he could be, this man surrounded by barriers and bodyguards. *Patience*. The word spoke volumes. "My patience with my grandpa puzzles you?"

"You run. He makes you go slow." He made his fingers walk the arm of the chair in slow steps.

Mari saw him again as she'd first seen him in the supermarket with his death grip on the cart, a man who barely moved at all while his mind traveled at warp speed. Oh, she could guess with whom he was impatient. She chose her words carefully. "You should not rate my patience too highly. It's an ordinary, imperfect sort of patience. I spend a little time with my grandpa a few afternoons a week. I'm not the one who had the stroke."

He gave a slight nod, and for the first time in their conversation, such as it was, he looked away, his gaze fixed on the view.

Outside it had grown dark. The streetlamps on the Strand glowed against the blackness. She got to her feet. The dog rose at his master's side. "You do know why people date, don't you?"

"Tell me," he said. One eyebrow actually arched upward. She realized how alert she was to his slightest movement.

"So they can discover things about each other, learn each other's tastes and values and histories, so they don't have to do Internet searches and compile dossiers on each other." She couldn't resist pointing out that he'd spied on her.

"You have questions you want me to answer."

"Yes." She was about to do something crazy. She could hear her friend Shanny already talking about red flags. The man was one giant flapping red flag. "If you…will answer my questions, I'll have dinner with you," she said. She *was* nuts.

He lowered his right hand to rest on the dog's head. "I will," he said.

Cinder Block appeared framed by a light beyond the darkened workout room. Mari hadn't detected any means of summoning him.

"Bradley will see you home."

Mari nodded and turned to Cinder Block. She had certainly not picked him for a Bradley.

"I'll send you a…plan, Maryrose," Jack said.

"You know where to reach me." She followed Bradley out of the room.

Chapter 4

At noon, Jack and his team picked up Huntington in Jack's specially fitted black SUV and, following the usual security precautions, drove out to the Palos Verdes peninsula. These days Huntington worked as a youth programs director for a storefront community center, serving the South Bay's less affluent citizens. It seemed out of character for the former trust fund golden boy, but Jack knew Huntington had a side most people never saw.

Jack left his chair in the car and used his walking sticks to navigate the uneven ground to a pair of boulders on the bluff looking back at the curving sweep of the Santa Monica Bay north to the distant hills of Malibu. Soldier settled at his feet. The sweat and nausea subsided. Waves crashed below the cliffs and a stiff breeze blew. Birds and rabbits disturbed the bushes. Distant runners passed.

"Congrats, man." Huntington settled beside him on another rock. "You're getting out of the chair more."

"Some."

"Any sign of the guy who came after you at the concert?"

"We're keeping watch. He'll be back."

"You have a plan, right? So that's not what's keeping you up at night. You look wasted."

"The woman." Jack had trained himself to relax, to lie perfectly still, to keep from unsettling the loose particles in the labyrinth of his inner ear that undid his balance, but after meeting Maryrose, he had been unable to turn off his brain. Or maybe it wasn't his brain. He hadn't thought about sex in a long time.

One of Huntington's golden brows lifted. "You met her already?"

Jack told the story, first of the supermarket encounter, and then of the meeting at the house. Huntington was a good listener and a patient one. He knew how Jack talked from the work they'd done together to launch Jack's project, a cross-platform video game for brain-injured vets. The game helped to retrain the brain for flexibility, and sales went to a foundation with more resources for vets. Jack's foundation had launched the game at a benefit concert in the spring featuring a reunion of the old metal group, Grindstone.

When Jack got to the part of his story about the details his team had collected about Maryrose Lynch and how he had planned to meet her under controlled conditions, Huntington laughed.

"It all went south, didn't it?"

"She just showed up."

"And shook you up. That's what the right kind of woman does, Ryker," Huntington said. "She spotted one of your guys and made the connection? Sounds scary smart."

Jack knew it. He liked how smart she was. Maybe that made her dangerous. She wanted to ask him questions. She wanted him to shake the habits he'd relied on to stay alive. From the moment he had dropped out of college, stopped being Jack Joyce and become Ryker, it had been his job to know as much as possible about the players in the room wherever an arms deal was going down from Tashkent to Abu Dhabi.

He owed his life to those habits and a group of marines. He was sitting free and alive on a cliff overlooking the Pacific because, even in captivity, he had studied his guards. He had discovered one, Ahmad, had a weakness for buying Western tech gadgets. He'd fed Ahmad info that led him to use one of Ryker's online payment accounts. The activity on his account had led the US authorities right to Jack. Not that the CIA or the DIA cared what became of Jack. He was just an asset, a man who had seen and could identify an elusive target who supplied terrorists with weapons. A platoon of marines had left an outpost on a rocky hillside and ventured into enemy territory to collect Jack. They had paid for that act of courage. The remaining members of that platoon made up Jack's team.

"So why did this woman stop outside your house?"

No surprise that Huntington picked up on an unexplained detail in Jack's story. Huntington paid attention. At Canyon, no one had given Huntington credit for his intelligence. It was easy to mistake Huntington's careless charm for a lack of brains, but even in high school, Jack had known that Huntington was more than the lazy golden boy he seemed to be. Huntington, like Sloan, had figured out how corrupt Headmaster Chambers was. Together in the past year, the three of them had brought Chambers down.

"She walks by the house with her grandfather."

"And?"

"The old man is Connor Lynch." Lynch reminded Jack of the veterans he'd met in the past two years. He told Huntington about the way Lynch grabbed the glass partition in front of Jack's patio and grew agitated whenever he passed. Jack recognized the pattern.

"You think the house is a trigger for the old man?"

"I do." The marine veterans Jack worked with now talked about those triggers, those moments when a movement at the corner of one's eye, an unexpected sound or smell could send a man into a hypervigilant state. It took a lot of work to learn to manage those triggers, to keep them from gaining the upper hand over one's actions and decisions. And knowing a little bit of Connor Lynch's history, his time in a Sinaloa prison, and knowing the history of the Strand house, Jack had an idea what Lynch's trigger was.

"Wait, the woman's name is Lynch, too? Who is she?"

"Maryrose Lynch." Jack liked saying her name, her old-fashioned name that suggested the things he'd seen in her already, her patience with her grandfather, and her mix of gentleness and fearlessness. Just her name sent his mind wandering a bit. He closed his eyes behind the dark glasses and let the salty ocean breeze wash over him. There was a simplicity about her. He liked how she looked in her vest and running pants. He liked her dark hair up, exposing the pale hollows at the base of her throat.

When he opened his eyes again, Huntington was holding out his phone with an image. "This Maryrose Lynch? The community relations director at the Coast Plaza Mall? I think she goes by 'Mari.'"

Jack found her in the middle of a group picture in front of the mall. She fit right in, looking polished and professional in a white linen jacket and slacks and as remote from a man like him as a woman could be. "Yes."

Huntington slipped the phone back into his pocket. "I talked with her this week. She's looking for Santas for Saturdays at the mall in the lead-up to Christmas. I tipped her off about one of the grandparents from the Center."

For a few minutes, Jack couldn't speak. Maybe the connection he felt with her was a delusion. He'd watched her for weeks, thinking he was getting to know her. The nickname made him think he'd been wrong about her patience and gentleness. Maybe she was worldly and businesslike.

One of the rabbits came out into the open, moving through the dry grass in short hops, stopping to nibble whatever it was rabbits nibbled, apparently indifferent to hawks overhead or Soldier at Jack's side. Soldier definitely took notice of the rabbit. A slight tremor ran through his body, and Jack put a steadying hand on his nape.

"She's going to have dinner with me," he said.

"Ah." Huntington's "ah" was expressive. "Where?"

"At the Strand house." Jack had to focus and make a plan. He was good at making plans, but his thoughts kept getting ahead of him.

"Smart move. The house could work. You're thinking of the upper deck? The sunset view."

"Yes."

"Your team will bring her there? I mean they're polite and all, but a bit on the big and scary side of normal." Huntington paused. He watched the horizon, not Jack. "Sloan and I, your friends, might be fine for a ride in one of your SUVs with a thousand pounds of wire-wearing muscle around us, but a girl who doesn't know you yet might be…intimidated."

"Security matters."

"So, you want to keep her safe. But not scare her away."

"Yes." Jack didn't pretend to misunderstand. Huntington had been present for the episode at the cross-platform video game launch concert when Jack and his marines had been targeted by his enemy. They'd been prepared with massive security and were lucky that time that Jack's enemy, Frank Evans, had sent a bungler who'd been picked up on security cameras before he could get to Jack. But Evans would make another attempt. Jack was counting on it and counting on his team as always to keep him and those around him safe. They'd managed to do it so far. He trusted them to keep doing it.

"Just dinner?"

Jack couldn't answer. Huntington was good at reading people. Jack might fool himself about what he wanted, but he wasn't fooling his friend.

Huntington rested a hand on Jack's shoulder. "It's that bad, is it? You're thinking ahead, but any…intimacy…that's got to be her call. Start with dinner. Let her know who you are. Coming from me, this is going to sound phony, but you can't eat the marshmallow. Patience, my friend, that's the key."

"Patience." The word almost choked him. When he first saw her, Jack thought he merely wanted to see her crack, see her lose patience with the old man's infirmities, the way Jack could lose patience. After he met her, after she challenged him, joked with him, looked at him and not at the chair, he lay awake in his bed in the dark, free of glasses and dizziness, and knew he wanted something else entirely from Maryrose Lynch.

The wandering rabbit ventured within a few yards of them. At Jack's feet, Soldier quivered with suppressed tension. Jack touched the dog's head and gave him the release command, and Soldier exploded into the field. For a few minutes, the ground was a blur of black dog, scrambling rabbit, flying bits of dry grass, and whirling dust. When the rabbit finally reached the deep brush that lined the cliff edge, Soldier trotted back and dropped, panting, at Jack's feet.

Jack had to get free of that chair.

***

On Thursday, Mari left her office to join her friend Shannon O'Rourke, one of the managers of the mall's indie bookstore, for a salad lunch in the food court. Mari wasn't yet used to calling it a food "hall," the latest thing.

A perky, compact blonde, Shannon drew smiles and greetings as she crossed the food court. Mari waved, and she had to laugh. She and Shanny, to her friends, had known each other since third grade. In sixth grade, Shanny had decided they needed matching nicknames and come up with "Mari" for Maryrose. What most people didn't know when they saw Shanny's perpetual smile was that Shanny couldn't resist a horror story. It was her habit to introduce a worst-case scenario into every conversation. She knew a friend or a friend of a friend who lost her life savings to a man she met online, or another whose pregnancy led to life-threatening surgery. She knew a couple who had been pursued by a polar bear in the Arctic on a kayaking trip and a woman whose rented Segway malfunctioned on her honeymoon and landed her in a foreign hospital for weeks. Shanny would make Jack into a full-on stalker for finding out who Mari was and where she lived. And Mari knew she didn't want that. Relying on her people instinct, not strict logic, she wanted to go ahead with their date.

The current plan was for Bradley, Jack's beefy security guy, to bring Mari to the house a little before sunset on Friday where Jack would be waiting. Bradley was definitely the scarier of the two men.

Mari had spent two sleepless nights overanalyzing the conversation in Jack's darkened workout room. Her instinct said that Jack had acted kind of like Shanny and Mari in high school, seeing a cute guy and finding out where his locker was and which parking space was his in the senior parking lot. Then logic would intrude, and Mari would remember all the things she didn't know about Jack, starting with his full name. The next instant her wide-awake brain would swing back to the fact that their meeting in the supermarket had been completely accidental, and finally, she had to admit that she'd been the one to barge into the fortress of a man who clearly had some major vulnerabilities to manage.

Shanny snagged a table in the crowded food court and placed her phone in easy reach while Mari picked up their preordered salads. The mall hadn't cued up the seasonal music yet, though management had announced the deadline for merchants to put up holiday-themed décor. In compliance some vendors had already draped garlands of fake greenery and dangling red and gold balls across their store fronts. A giant mechanical turkey bobbed its wooden head near the opening of the food court. Shoppers could ascend a short ramp, lift a red flap in the turkey's feathers, and drop canned goods into the turkey's body for the annual food drive.

"How's the Santa search?" Shanny opened her boxed Ahi salad.

"Almost done. Two more interviews lined up." Mari favored the chicken-walnut salad. It felt particularly virtuous to be eating salads in the crosscurrent of aromas from the cinnamon bun shop and the pizza place.

"Any of them good enough to be your Saturday Santa?"

"One possibility. And I could use your help. I've got a Black Santa lined up."

Shanny's brows went up. "Good for you. How's the big boss like that?"

Mari hadn't broached the subject with her boss yet. She thought he'd go for it. He might not be as committed to diversity as the corporate mission statement declared, but he was into sales volume. Black Santas were a big draw in several East Coast and Midwest malls. "He's going to be okay with it, I think. But could you do a window display with some of the kids' books that feature Black Santas?"

"Great idea." Shanny bounced a little in her seat. "I know some lovely books." She picked up her phone and showed Mari a cover. "This is one of my favorites. Cute, huh?"

"Perfect. Thanks."

"But nobody's as good a Santa as your grandpa, right? How is he?" Shanny knew Grandpa Connor well from times on his boat when they were in middle school and, more recently, before his stroke when he'd come to her store as Santa to read at a story hour for preschoolers.

"Abby's got him under lock and key at the moment. He's been a little agitated on our walks lately."

"She's not pushing you all to put him in a care facility, is she? You know Joan Pappas." As Mari nodded, Shanny poured the last of her dressing onto her salad. "She almost lost her grandmother in one of those places. I mean, her grandmother just went in after hip surgery. It was supposed to be for twenty-one days. And…"

Mari ate her chicken as Shanny detailed the story of Joan's grandmother's near-death experience from infection and neglect in a rehab facility. Eventually, Joan's grandmother recovered, and Shanny's story came to an end. "You look a little down, Mari."

"Actually, Shanny, I have to bail for tomorrow night. I'm sorry."

"Tomorrow? But it's Irish Music Night." Shanny didn't do online dating. Her theory was that a woman picked an activity she enjoyed doing and stuck with it. Someone who liked the same music or the same sport was bound to have a single friend or a single brother or a single friend of a friend. The monthly Irish Music Night at the Fireside, an old tavern on the Coast Highway, was Shanny's thing, and Mari usually joined her. Shanny, a proud graduate of female self-defense classes, never went anywhere without a "wingman." A woman couldn't be too careful.

"I'm sorry, Shanny. I met this…person. I wasn't expecting him to ask me…out, but…"

"But he did. Well, that's okay." Shanny picked up her phone. "Let me just text Erin. Maybe she can be my wingman. Who is this guy, by the way?"

Mari stabbed another forkful of lettuce and chicken. "He's not online. We collided, literally, in the supermarket. His cart broke my eggs, and he sent me new ones."

"Sweet. He's sweet, then. Is he cute?"

"Very attractive." Mari stuck to the unproblematic things about Jack. She didn't want Shanny thinking Jack was a stalker. True, Jack had discovered where she lived, but sending a carton of eggs was hardly the act of a creep.

Shanny's phone pinged, and she checked the text. "You meeting him for coffee? Drinks?"

"Dinner." Mari kept her gaze on her greens.

Shanny's eyes widened. "Ooh, so he doesn't mind paying. That's good. But dinner… Could be a long evening if he's a loser. What did you say he does?"

"I don't know. Money is no object, apparently."

Shanny, of course, noticed the evasion. She put down her fork. "Did you do a search, check him out in the usual places?"

"No. Just trying to get to know him by…talking." Mari had had hours to compare Jack to her carefully constructed profile of the sort of man she wanted to meet. Her ideal man was supposed to be fit, funny, and smart; employed, educated, and eligible. Nowhere did she list mysterious, taciturn, and intense.

Shanny shook her head. "Nothing wrong with conversation, Mari, but you wouldn't hire a Santa without a background check, right?"

"He's solvent, at least. He has a house on the Strand." As soon as she said it, Mari knew she'd handed Shanny too much information.

Shanny went right to her phone. "Ooh, the Strand, huh. Address?"

Mari shrugged and dropped her compostable fork and napkin in the empty salad box. She didn't want Shanny to start searching for Jack's fortress house. "North end somewhere."

Shanny stopped her scrolling. "What are you not telling me about your guy, Mari?"

"He's not 'my guy,' Shanny. I just met him. We're going to have dinner, not sex." Mari stood. "I've got to get back to work. A million things to do to make Christmas 2015 a blockbuster, you know." She parodied her boss's usual hyperbole.

"Okay. Nothing like retail at Christmas." Shanny gathered up her lunch things and slid her phone into her jacket pocket. "I hope this guy likes Christmas, because you do Christmas twenty-four-seven."

"I'll have to ask him." One more question for her list.

They crossed the crowded food court and tossed their salad boxes into the appropriate bin. Shanny wanted to know what Mari planned to wear.

"That blue wrap dress."

"The batiky-looking one."

"That works." Shanny stopped. "Just don't get sucked in, okay? Some guys are such smooth talkers, you know."

"I won't." Mari kept a straight face. She might get sucked in, but it wouldn't be because of Jack's verbal charms.

Shanny looked skeptical. "Try to think like your grandpa. He could always spot a phony, and if anything's not right, you bail at once. Ditch him and text me, okay?"

***

Mari's first impression was that Jack was a fan of the new tidying-up craze. In the second-story living room, there were no rugs on the wide-planked wood floor. No art hung on the gray walls; no books lined the shelves. There were no shelves, only a charcoal-colored sectional sofa in one corner.

Her next impression wiped out all thoughts of décor. Jack stood with the dog at his side, dressed as he'd been in the supermarket: a deep blue plaid surfer shirt over khakis with flip-flops on his beautiful feet and dark glasses hiding his eyes. He was taller and broader shouldered than she remembered, but as arrestingly still, as symmetrically aligned.

Beyond him stood a table set for two in front of the floor-to-ceiling windows with their view of the ocean. Glassware and silver gleamed. A faint tropical fragrance wafted her way from a white blossom floating in a glass bowl. Jack's black chair was drawn up at one end, and a similar chair at the other. Through the windows, the low sun shed a soft, diffused light over the sand, the surge and ebb of the waves, the foam and glittering crests, and the bobbing surfers and swooping birds.

"If you are trying to wow me, it's working," she said.

The tiniest movement of his lips suggested that she had won his low-key version of a smile. "You like it."

She nodded. "I still have questions," she reminded him. "That was the deal."

He stretched out a hand to her, palm up. She stepped forward and put her hand in his. His thumb brushed over the fading line of the gash on the tops of her fingers, and the sexual punch of him hit her hard. She stared up into his hidden eyes, trying to see whether he felt what she did.

Behind them, someone made a deep, throat-clearing noise, and Mari turned to find a large man dressed in a white shirt and black slacks standing beside the door. Jack released her hand, and her brain came out of its daze. *A waiter*. A waiter was good. A waiter meant she and Jack could not simply fling themselves on the corner sofa and have sex.

This particular waiter was more like a bouncer at a club than any waiter she'd ever seen, and like Bradley, who'd brought her to Jack and collected her phone at the door, the man wore an earbud and a wire. She smiled politely as he came forward and let him offer her a seat and a glass of wine. In the few seconds consumed by the business, she missed seeing how Jack negotiated his chair. It was no ordinary chair, but she didn't know why he needed it. She realized the waiter had been a deliberate distraction, a reminder that whatever the state of her host's body, his mind was quick. She would focus on that.

They sat at opposite ends of the small table by the window. Jack's glass matched hers, but not his beverage.

"You don't drink?" she asked.

"Not alcohol." He raised his glass to hers, and she tilted hers to meet it. The rims of their glasses touched, and a shiver went through Mari. She turned resolutely to the sunset and sipped her wine. This was bad. She was alone with a powerfully attractive man who was short-circuiting her brain. Most of the men in her life were colleagues, relatives, friends—people she talked to or worked with every day. Ordinary men, not enigmatic strangers. Some of them were very nice to look at, but none of them made her feel an immediate imperative to contribute to the planet's population. The sofa made a mockery of her easy assurance to Shanny that she wasn't going to sleep with Jack.

"You have questions," he said.

She squared her shoulders. She'd agreed to this date because he wasn't like the men she'd been meeting. He didn't radiate self-importance as they did, and she guessed he had no idea of his attractiveness. "Oh, I do. Are you wearing your bulletproof vest?"

Again, she thought his lips made a faint smile. He pressed his hand flat on his chest. "Ready," he said.

"Why were you in the supermarket?" She'd thought about it a lot. "You have staff, Internet access, money, and a very strong desire for privacy. You can't tell me you were stopping on your way home from work to pick up a few items."

He set down his glass and rested a hand on the dog's head, his thumb stroking the dog's ear. "Training," he said.

The choreographed scene of his leaving the supermarket replayed in her mind. His answer made sense. The mall had recently run its employees through the required yearly emergency drills, and Mari knew all the exits and hiding places available and how to signal employees to secure their stores.

The waiter returned pushing a rolling cart with covered dishes. He set about placing plates of salad, grilled fish, and rolls in front of them. The food looked beautiful and smelled delicious, but she wasn't ready to eat. A tattoo on the waiter's arm caught her eye, an image of the boots and helmet of a fallen marine hung on a cross of the man's rifle. She'd seen the real thing when friends of her parents had buried a son. Bradley had the same image on his arm.

The waiter vanished. With the sound of the door shutting, Mari sensed that the living room with its magnificent ocean view was sealed off from the outside. Air moved gently, but no sound reached them from the Strand below or the beach beyond it.

"Your staff… Were they, are they marines?" she asked.

"Yes."

"You?"

"No." In the absence of other sounds, his voice had a texture. Self-deprecating didn't begin to describe him.

She took another sip of wine. He'd spared no expense. She recognized the high-end Pinot from a wine tasting at an upscale restaurant next to the mall. "In your former life, were you in the hospitality business?"

"Former life?"

She'd caught him off guard. "Before you became a professional recluse."

There was a slight tightening of his jaw. "My mother liked room service."

Maryrose noted the past tense. "Your dad?"

"Gone."

She wanted to ask who they had been and what they had done and whether they had other children who were less wounded than the man in front of her. He had told her he had three friends, counting the dog. He had a higher count of losses, apparently. She turned to the window and the sinking sun, orange-tinged in the slight haze of the November sky. In a few minutes, the glowing ball would touch the horizon. Conditions were perfect for the green flash phenomenon her Grandpa Connor had taught her to look for.

"Hungry?" Jack asked. There was a hint of what—vulnerability—in the question. "The halibut is local."

He'd taken pains, or hired people to take pains, to please her, a fisherman's daughter, and it was a lovely meal. She picked up her fork and tried the fish. For a few minutes, she ate and watched the sun's downward progress with only surreptitious glances at Jack. She forgot her questions in a protracted moment of admiring the clean line of his jaw and the column of his throat and wondering about the tattoos hidden by the longish hair hanging in lazy curls to his collar. If he was eating, he wasn't eating much. The chair and the service dog, the gaps in his careful speech, surely meant some form of impairment? He didn't fit any of the categories she could name, except, perhaps, PTSD, but that didn't seem right.

She put down her fork. "Tell me about your dog. How long has he been with you?"

"Soldier? Two years." Jack broke a roll open and put it down. His movements precise, deliberate.

"Where did he come from?"

Mari thought he wouldn't answer as he picked up and put down a butter knife.

"My team found him."

She switched to water. She was getting used to his way of leaving gaps for her to fill in. *Team* was an interesting term, since he seemed to be the one giving orders. "You mean Bradley and the others? How many…?"

"Eight."

There was something in the way he said it that alerted her. "Because you lost…?"

He held up two fingers.

"Where?"

"Afghanistan."

More losses. The country's name conjured images from news accounts to which she hadn't paid enough attention. She knew next to nothing about Afghanistan. It was mountainous. Its people had seen continuous war since the Russian invasion and the arrival of US forces after 9/11. She had a vague idea that Afghanistan had once been a garden place of pomegranates and apricots, but that now its fields were often planted with land mines and IEDs. A whole new train of questions arose. If he wasn't a soldier, what had he been doing in Afghanistan?

"Ten questions," he said.

She smiled and raised her glass to him. She wasn't at all finished with her questions. "You're doing really well."

"My turn," he said. He leaned forward a little.

"Your turn?" she asked.

"You said people date to find out…about each other. How did you get your name?"

"My full name, you mean? The usual Irish way. My parents put two aunts together, Aunt Mary and Aunt Rose."

"You were teased."

He was right, but Mari was sure his Internet search had turned up no record of the humiliations of her first year in middle school. "What makes you think that?"

One of his dark brows quirked slightly upward. "I went to high school."

"I'm astonished. How ordinary of you. Where?"

"Canyon."

It took her awhile to interpret his answer. She'd heard the school's name recently or read about it in the paper. There had been a scandal. "The boys school?"

"Yes." He watched her from behind his glasses. "Your name's a nun's name—Sister Maryrose."

"That's why my friends call me Mari." She picked up her wineglass and turned back to the sun. He really was too smart for her. Maybe his glasses were not a fashion accessory, but a necessity, a cover for some injury he'd sustained, but it was unfair of him to hide behind them. Next time she'd wear her own dark glasses. "What did they call you? At Canyon?"

The sun's lower rim touched the horizon where sea and sky met. Again she thought he wouldn't answer.

"The Invisible Man." His steady, indifferent baritone didn't waver. Maybe the pain of an old joke didn't matter anymore.

Mari put down her wineglass. The whole point was to get answers out of him, to gain some control of the situation, but his answers kept deepening the mystery. She definitely needed to lighten the subject. "Do you watch the sunset often?"

"Most days," he said. "You walk most days."

A flash of awareness washed over her. He was admitting the intensity of his interest in her. She concentrated on the sun. The bright ball began to shimmer and shift, melting into liquid bars of gold, its rays blazing a glittering path on the waves. What had seemed a slow descent became a rapid slide as if a video were fast-forwarded. She waited for the green flash and almost missed what he said next.

"I know why."

"Why what?" She turned to him. His beautiful face was serious.

"Your grandpa reacts to this house."

"What?"

"He went to prison because of this house. In Mexico when you were…eight."

"Grandpa Connor? No." Mari shook her head. Jack wasn't making sense. "Grandpa Connor would never…. He… What are you talking about?"

She sensed his unwavering attention behind the dark glasses.

"Mexican agents boarded his boat in Baja. There was cocaine."

"My grandpa? With drugs on his boat? Never. Why are you saying such a thing?"

"The man who owned this house laundered money for a cartel. I think the house is a trigger for your grandpa."

Mari stared at the man opposite her with his beautiful mouth and hidden eyes. He spoke slowly, deliberately, whole sentences now, not the pixels of information he'd released about himself. And one thing was painfully clear: this hadn't been a date. It had been some kind of probe into her life, and he'd taken it way too far.

"You investigated him, too? My grandfather? You conceal everything about yourself and compile dossiers about everyone else?" She pushed back in her chair, reached for her bag, and realized Bradley had it and her phone. "I have to go now. You can signal your team or whatever it is you do." She stood. She was shaking with anger and a sudden chill. The sun was down. "Thank you for a lovely dinner. Let's not do it again."

"Wait." He gripped the chair arm, and with a slight mechanical whir, the chair rolled back and swung away from the table. Mari couldn't look away. Soldier came to his feet, and Jack pushed up from his seat. Too late, she took a step back, and he reached for her, snagging her hand in his. She tried to pull free, and he let go, stumbling, dropping to his knees and pitching forward. His hands smacked the floor, stopping his fall, and the glasses tumbled from his face.

Mari froze. Her breath caught in her throat. Her heart contracted painfully. One minute he made her furious with his invasion of her life, his spying, the next she couldn't bear to cause him pain.

She sank to the floor, facing him, on her knees too. Soldier made a menacing sound in his throat. Her own throat felt suddenly raw.

"Soldier, down," he commanded.

The dog obeyed.

Mari gathered Jack's fallen glasses and held them in her lap. She remembered him gripping the shopping cart. Now he appeared to be steadying himself by some supreme effort of will against whatever shook his whole frame. The dog licked his hand. Jack rocked back in a smooth move, so that he sat, his hands resting on his thighs, eyes closed.

"I'm still here," she said. "I have your glasses in my hand." His breathing slowed, a practiced effort at calming himself, his only movement a slight flaring of his nostrils. In the shadows and without the glasses, his harsh face, taut with concentration, was more striking than ever.

No one came. He hadn't summoned them. His shoulders relaxed as he opened his eyes, and Mari fell into them. The glasses had misled her. There was nothing wrong with his eyes. They were deep pools of darkness, surrounded by a rim of vivid blue. She could think only of the huge eyes of abandoned children in refugee camps clinging to chain-link fences, but he was a man, not a child, and the unguardedness of his eyes must have been only the natural dilation caused by sitting in darkness.

"I thought you'd want to know," he said.

It took her a long beat to realize he meant that she'd want to know about her grandfather's past, the reason for his agitation whenever he saw Jack's house.

She nodded. What he said about her grandpa couldn't be true, but she could acknowledge that there was another side to the story: Jack's side.

Chapter 5

Mari sat on Jack's living room floor in the fading light, her skirts around her, Jack's dark glasses in her cupped hands on her lap. One minute she wanted to hit him—he made her so angry with his searching into her life and her grandpa's life, digging up ugliness and lies—the next minute she ached with pain for him, for whatever had left him broken.

"I blew it," he said.

It was an acknowledgment, if not exactly an apology. "Accusing my grandpa of drug dealing was a bit of a mood wrecker. You don't do a lot of…dating, do you?"

He held up his thumb and forefinger, less than half an inch apart.

"That much, huh?" She studied his glasses in her hands. There had to be a reason he lived as he did. There must be a story behind the bodyguards, the closed-circuit TV, and the social blunders. She looked up at him again. "Let's start over. Hi. My name is Mari Lynch. What's yours?"

"Ryker. Jack Ryker."

The harsh-sounding name sent a little shiver through her. "What do you do for fun, Jack Ryker?"

"Fun?"

She'd surprised him. "Let me explain the concept. Amusement. Entertainment. Recreation. Another reason to date."

His beautiful mouth gave its tiny spasm of a smile. "Pleasure. Diversion. Delight?"

"Good. You get the idea. Do you go out in the world? It's dangerous in here."

"That sofa worries you?" He gave the sofa a slow, sliding glance that made her pulse skip. He had felt what she'd felt.

"No." She denied it. "Not a bit worried about it. There's a waiter and probably cameras."

"I can turn them off."

"There are cameras?" Her voice squeaked a little. "You mean there's footage of our dinner? Our conversation?"

"Tonight, no cameras." He glanced at the sofa again. "In case…"

"In case?" A shivery laugh shook her. Her breasts tightened in reaction to the low, rough timbre of his voice. "You're an optimist, then."

"A…planner." His gaze dropped, his dark lashes veiling his expression.

"You don't do public places, though, do you?"

It was one of those moments when her question seemed to have taken a wrong turn down some endless corridor in his brain. At last Soldier licked his hand, and he spoke. "I prefer not to."

"Are you part of a sensory deprivation experiment? No light, no sound?"

"It helps," he said.

There it was: another oblique but matter-of-fact reference to his impairment. Mari let out a long breath. The room had grown cold. If she'd ever had a buzz from the wine, it had faded. There was nothing more to say. The sensible thing to do was to end the evening. They weren't a good match. Maybe they both felt a strong sexual attraction, but she was all about family, friends, and being connected, and he was…not. "I really must go. This time of year. In retail. We're very busy." She rushed the words as if hurrying them could get her up and out the door, but the pull of him held her in place. He noticed.

"You like it."

"Retail? It is…what it is. I love Christmas, though. You?"

He looked down, settling his hand on the dog's head. "Haven't done it in a while."

"How long?"

"Too long."

It was an evasion, not a direct answer like his others. More evidence of the absence of family in his life. "Can you stand?"

"Yes." His mouth was a grim line.

She waited. He leaned forward, put his hands on the floor, and with a quick flex of his arms, rocked back onto his feet. He remained coiled for a moment, then straightened slowly, almost like a dancer, unfolding upward, and stood with closed eyes. For a moment she thought he might topple, as if he were imperfectly balanced like the last block on one of her toddler nephew's piles that could bring down the whole structure. When he opened his eyes again, she, too, stood and reached out to offer him the glasses. Their fingers touched. Instead of taking the glasses, his hand closed around her wrist, and he pulled her into his arms. She laid her head against his chest and leaned into his solid warmth, her ear pressed to the flap of his shirt pocket. His arms came around her, his hands pressed to her back, each of his fingers distinct through the thin jersey of her dress.

"When can I see you again?" he asked.

It was a crazy question, yet she had wanted this contact, to be pressed against him, from the moment she'd walked in the door. He held her lightly, the way one held a trapped bird. It would have been easy to pull away if she had the will for it. He was all wrong for her. They should not meet again.

"You didn't ask all your questions," he said, his hold loosening.

She twisted in his arms to look up at him. He wanted to keep going.

A wild idea occurred to her, about as smart as standing in tall grass, lighting matches. She didn't have to walk away. She would simply set conditions so that he could. "Meet me at the mall food court for lunch tomorrow."

His expression turned comically dismayed.

"That's your worst nightmare, isn't it?"

"Torture," he said. "Food courts violate the Geneva Conventions."

"I understand," she said. "I won't be offended if you don't come, and thank you again for tonight." She meant it. She stepped back, and his hold slid away. She willed herself not to miss the warmth of him. She offered the glasses, and this time he took them. With a smile, she turned for the door. Heavy footsteps approached from the other side. In a minute she'd be gone. It would be over.

"What about Monday?" he said.

She stopped and spun back to him, stunned by the sudden way the words lifted her spirits. "Monday?"

"It takes planning," he said. "I'll be there."

The door opened behind her, letting in light from the hall, but leaving Jack Ryker in the dark.

"Ms. Lynch, I'll take you home now." Old Cinder Block Bradley stood at the door with her bag in hand.

***

Jack's team met around the big pine kitchen table after breakfast. Everyone had a mug of coffee and stared glumly at a detailed site map of the mall spread out on the table. So far Jack's plan to meet Mari Lynch in the food court had not won a big thumbs-up from the guys. Jack let them speak. Since he was asking them to keep her safe too, they deserved to have their say.

They were all there except Miguel, who had morning perimeter duty. No one said a word about Mari Lynch. Meeting her was the first thing in two years that Jack wanted to do apart from the mission, but against their claim on him, his desire to see her meant next to nothing.

Jack had insisted from the beginning when he'd recruited them for the mission that beating their elusive enemy was about control. They'd taught him that it was also about trust. Together they controlled Jack's house, every approach, every entrance and exit covered. Together they'd worked and waited two years to trap an enemy who had a dozen names and looked as plain as white bread. Frank Evans was of medium height, with sandy-colored hair, no sharp distinguishing features, and a habit of making subtle changes to his appearance. The FBI didn't know how many passports he had. He slipped in and out of the country with ease. He had perfected being forgettable as he crossed borders. But Jack couldn't forget him or mistake him.

For years, Evans had cultivated ties to important people in the American intel community while making deals with enemies of the US. He knew his way around the government's black budget and the global surveillance market where various militaries sought to buy high-tech advantages over their enemies or their own people. And three years earlier, he'd been willing to trade the lives of a group of American marines in order to demonstrate a surveillance product and win a deal for a client in Tashkent. As far as Jack knew, Evans had not done any deals since he'd realized that Jack could identify him. That would make Evans desperate by now.

Jack watched his team. Everything he knew about being on a team came from working with them. Each had a distinct energy, but each was part of the whole.

Nick, wiry and edgy, circled the big kitchen table. He hated Jack's plan to meet Mari in the mall. He didn't want to lose patience and make a mistake.

Marcus, Jack's head of security and waiter from the night before, watched Nick warily. The two of them had been together the longest of the team. "We almost got Evans, not at the house, but at the Grindstone concert where Jack made himself a target. Maybe our best shot at Evans comes when Jack makes himself a target again."

"Right," said Rashaad from the foot of the table. He was the even-tempered one of the team. "Jack has always been the target. He's the bait in the trap."

Bradley spoke next. "We controlled the environment at the concert, and Evans sent a proxy in ahead of him to spring the trap. We got the proxy, but not Evans."

Nick stopped his circling of the table and turned to Jack. "Will you use the chair? If Evans shows up and you're puking your guts out before you're halfway down the mall, you'll never see him coming."

"Seeing Evans is on us," said Rashaad. "That's our job."

"I still don't like it," Bradley said. "We did our job at the concert in May, and no one got hurt, but security in a place like this—" He tapped the floor plan on the table. "—is gonna be a joke. What about collateral damage if Evans shows up?"

There was a long moment of silence. They all knew about collateral damage. Their buddies Vince and Hank were dead. They had scars and injuries. Miguel had one less leg, and Rashaad had friends still in the service, still at risk from their enemy and men like him.

"It's me he wants," Jack said. It was Jack who had been in the room at Camp Dwyer Combat Support Hospital in southern Afghanistan, going through his pre-release debrief. At the time, over two years earlier, after his rescue, he couldn't sit up, couldn't move his head, but he could hear, and he never forgot a voice. "No one else."

Jack's trainer Cole, the newest member of the team, spoke up. "Jack managed the supermarket without the chair. I say he's ready to go, but he has to take the dog."

"And he's gotta wear a wire." Nick directed a sharp glare at Jack. "And memorize the effing floor plan. That's nonnegotiable. Let Marcus and I do a recon before it's a go."

Rashaad nodded. He turned to Jack and fixed him with a long, steady look. Under that level gaze, a person couldn't lie to Rashaad or to himself. "The team says 'leave,' you leave, right, man? You get up and walk, right? Woman or no woman. You let us do our job."

Jack gave a thumbs-up sign.

***

Mari arrived at her mom and dad's house in the early evening winter darkness. Streetlights and porch lights glowed in the old neighborhood, yet the brightest light streamed from her family's open double-car garage out onto the sloping driveway packed with four cars. She headed for the garage and accepted greetings and hugs from her aunts and cousins and sisters-in-law. Her Aunt Mary handed her an apron and a pair of rubber gloves. Tools and fishing gear lined the walls of her dad's domain, but where the cars normally sat stood two picnic tables pushed together end-to-end and covered in newspaper. Piled at one end of the long expanse were silver serving items—trays, flatware, urns, sugar bowls, and gravy boats in various stages of coming untarnished. It was "Silver-Polishing Sunday" at the Lynch house, an annual pre-Thanksgiving event organized by Mari's mother, Ruth.

Mari took her place in the assembly line of Lynch women. She dipped a sponge into an open jar of pink goo and set to work on a sugar bowl. Her mom waved from the other end of the tables, where she supervised two of the younger cousins, who manned tubs of warm soapy water and wielded drying cloths. Inside the house, the male members of the Lynch clan—husbands, brothers, uncles, and grandsons—would be watching football in the den, while in the kitchen her dad prepared venison stew from the Lynch brothers' annual deer-hunting expedition north of Mendocino.

With so much family around her, it now struck her as odd that she couldn't remember her grandpa ever being there. After the divorce, it had been his habit to see his grandchildren on the other side of the hill. Mari had been unable to forget Jack Ryker's troubling accusation. It made her wonder if there wasn't something more to Grandpa Connor's inevitable absence from family gatherings. She made up her mind to ask her father about it when he took a break from his cooking duties.

She liked being busy. She liked preparing for Christmas. It made no sense that she couldn't stop thinking about Jack Ryker. She hardly knew him. He was a control freak who had pried in the most troubling way into her life and her grandfather's, yet his bleak surroundings baffled her. There were no bits of memorabilia, no treasured possessions of sentimental value, and not a single photograph. His house was a blank, as if he had no past, but he clearly did. His tattooed neck, his mechanical chair, his dog, his personal security guards spoke of a past remote from hers. Thinking of him set her body humming with unexpressed sexual energy. Her traitorous brain defended him. He could be funny and smart. He was wounded. His dog loved him. He could smile that faint whisper of a smile. He made no secret of wanting her.

Her second cousin, Betty, nudged her to give up the sugar bowl and move on to another piece, and Mari emerged from the fog of her thoughts about Jack. She had lots of family news to catch up on.

Between games, her dad finally strolled from the house in his black chef's apron. "Stew's ready," he announced. There was a general bustle, a putting away of silver paste and sponges as people began to move toward the house. Mari screwed the lid back on her tub of pink goo and pulled off her rubber gloves, watching until she found her dad standing alone on the lawn, with a beer in hand. She crossed to his side.

"Hi, honey," he said. "How's retail treating you?"

"It's crazy."

"Are you bringing someone home to meet us at Thanksgiving this year?"

"I…" She cast him a glance. "Where did you get that idea?"

Her dad shrugged a bit too casually and swigged the last of his beer. "Just wondering."

"Was Shanny here?"

He grinned. "Your mom's ready to set an extra place at the table."

"Dad, I just met this man. Premature to think about bringing him home."

Her dad threw an arm around her shoulders and offered her a squeeze. He smelled like onions and salsa, chips and beer. “We can hope.”

“Dad, can I ask you a question about Grandpa Connor?”

Her dad’s grin faded instantly. He pulled back, and she sensed his wariness. “Funny topic to bring up. Why do you want to ask about him?”

“I just wondered why he’s never been part of anything since…the divorce. Was it really so bad?”

Her dad didn’t look at her. “I know he’s your hero. Let’s just say, he’s not mine. He made a choice about this family a long time ago.”

“What choice?” Mari had a sudden sinking feeling that Jack had spoken the truth, a truth that had been there all along, lurking around the edges of family gatherings for years, never permitted to enter.

“Never mind. It was a long time ago. Water under the dam. We’ve survived.”

“Dad, I’m twenty-eight, not eight.” She took a deep breath. “Was Grandpa ever arrested?”

Her dad’s startled gaze swung back to her. “Who told you?”

“He *was* arrested.”

Her dad’s stricken face confirmed it. He took a long time to answer, not looking at her, rubbing his thumb around the rim of his beer glass. “I’ll never understand it. Maybe he was unhappy, but he sure went off the deep end. You might as well know. He took the boat to Baja to pick up dope for some big-shot lawyer from your side of the hill. The boat, our boat. We lost it. Everything we’d saved and worked for. We almost lost the house. Your mom had to work. And he just…walked away.”

The night was actually cold for LA, and Mari shivered with the chill. “He went to jail.”

“In Mexico. He needed lawyers, lots of lawyers. Another hole to pour money into. It took three years to get him out.”

“And then?”

Her dad straightened. “He said he’d make it up to us, get it all back, but I was angry. I didn’t want his help. Your uncle Dan and I, we figured it out, got loans, got going again. And your grandpa went back to his life as if he hadn’t screwed up ours. I still get angry about it. It was dumb. It was reckless. It was some kind of sting, and that lawyer knew it.”

Mari put her arms around her dad, who had never done a dumb or reckless thing that she knew of, and offered a hug. After a brief hesitation, he hugged her back. She couldn't take it in. Her grandpa had nearly ruined his family. She'd never guessed. She'd only seen the grandpa she adored, had not imagined that any other version of Connor Lynch existed. The absences and the silences made sense. "I'm sorry I brought it up, Dad," she said, "especially today. I didn't know the story."

Her dad gave her a squeeze and pulled away. "I know," he said. "The old man's been your 'Saturday Santa' for a long time. I didn't want you to know."

Chapter 6

Jack worked his way down the mall's main passage. He had to agree with his team: mall security was a joke. Evans would love the place. The random, shifting movement of the crowd made it easy for a person to blend in or fade out of notice at will. Even a non-pro could spot the overhead cameras aimed at store entrances and avoid them. In the wide center passageway, arrangements of oversize patio furniture, recycling bins, and potted trees offered plenty of concealment. The uniformed guards on patrol were a friendly lot, more like party hosts than an armed deterrent to crime. Jack passed one of them, tall and blond, sipping cider from a tiny paper cup while chatting up an aproned employee of a high-end kitchenware shop.

Getting his bearings in the place was like staring into a stream, trying to catch objects through the veil of rapidly moving water. It was one thing to memorize a still shot of the layout—he'd done that—it was another to experience the mall full of moving shoppers. Too much noise, too many lights blinking and flickering. The constant, irregular motion taxed his senses. The dark glasses helped, but his brain struggled to sort out and assess random stimuli. He already had the cold sweats and the first hint of nausea. At his side, Soldier was a steady presence. People gave them room, responding to Soldier's vest and harness, signs of a working service dog.

Jack had taken so much for granted—the ordinary, simple pleasure of movement, of standing securely on two legs. He'd never considered walking a luxury. He had assumed that old age was his future, his distant future, even at the height of demand for his consulting services. In those days, he could do a takedown and reassemble a rifle in under a minute with his eyes closed and explain the ergonomics and reliability of a dozen variations of the AR-15/M16/M4 platform right down to the best weapon for a decent cheek weld, and the only one that could handle desert sand, fine-grained like talcum powder.

He had had the arrogance to think he could remain untouched by the job, an arrogance he had probably learned at Canyon. At school he'd been small as a first-year student, and his classmates had taken advantage of his size to stuff him in trash cans or lock him in the big dictionary cupboards in the Hall of Canyon Men. He'd always escaped. Much later, when he'd grown into his height, he had believed himself untouched by the weapons around him. He never used them. Unless a man had a team, like Jack's team, a man with a gun in his hand often became a mere extension of the gun, part of the thing, subject to its purpose not his own.

He stopped where the two long branches of the mall met at a sunken circular gathering area two steps below the main walkway. Surfaces of sleek, polished stone in pale colors curved in patterns like dry creek beds in the flooring. Water flowed over the hidden edge of a low, shimmering pool. To Jack's right, Rashaad looked at a display in a bookstore window, using the reflection like a car's rearview mirror. Below, Bradley sat at a metal table with a paper coffee cup and an open laptop. On the opposite side of the gathering space, Nick sat on a bench, looking at his phone. Jack was covered. He waited another beat. Then Marcus emerged from across the food court, strolling around the perimeter, a folded newspaper under his arm. It was the *okay* signal. There was an escape route to Miguel parked in one of the team's SUVs behind the mall.

With Soldier's help, Jack negotiated the two stairs down into the food court. It was more of a food hall: the new concept of upscale food concession. Still, a sharp wave of nausea hit his empty stomach as the mingled aromas of competing cuisines swirled around him. The air was full of shawarma, Thai fusion, poke, pulled pork, espresso, and cinnamon-sugar-coated bread. Chairs scraped the floor underfoot, jarring voices blasted his ears, and the bass track of the piped-in music vibrated in his uneasy gut. He made it to an unoccupied chair with a view of the exit and of a giant wooden turkey painted in autumn colors, surrounded by a wooden platform and ramp. A sign read—Donate Canned Goods Here. The turkey's head bobbed in a steady rhythm, and Jack focused on that regular movement, concentrating, letting the other stimuli fade into the background. He could feel Soldier relax as Jack got his overloaded senses under control.

He was pretty sure he was past the threat of puking when he saw Mari coming across the food court.

She waved and came straight for him. An ordinary guy would leap up and pull out a seat for her. He hoped she would ignore the rudeness. She looked tired, hassled, and beautiful in dark wool slacks and some kind of sweater pair in a rich caramel color. The thin leather strap of her bag crossed her chest between her breasts. He had a visceral recollection of holding her pressed against him three nights before. She took the chair opposite him and closed her eyes, giving a little shake of her head, as if to clear her mind.

“Excuse me,” she said, opening her eyes. “Busy day.” She smiled, her hands clasped lightly together, resting on the little table, within his reach, but in a classic business-meeting position that put him on his guard. She looked polished and aloof, not like the woman he’d watched from his window gently holding her grandfather’s hand.

“I’m glad you came.” She gave him a direct look and squared her shoulders. “I want to apologize.”

“Just apologize?”

“You were right about my grandpa.” As soon as she said it, she looked vulnerable again, her dark eyes troubled. “I thought he was one kind of person. He was my ‘Saturday Santa’ here at the mall. I never even did the usual checks on him. No one background checks their grandpa, right? I believed he was the man he seemed to be. I made him this ideal, not an actual person. He was my standard of kindness and patience and generosity.”

“Now he’s not?” Jack hadn’t told her about her grandpa’s prison time to disillusion or hurt her.

She dropped her gaze to her clasped hands and her voice sank. “I feel dumb, like I’ve been played.” She paused. He could sense her searching for words. She was careful to say what she meant, and he liked that about her. “It’s strange to feel that loving someone, trusting them was dumb. He hurt my dad, my family, in ways I never realized. He could have told me, but he never did. I guess that’s the worst of it.”

“Why do you think he did it?” Jack watched the top of her head, waiting for the question to sink in.

"My dad thinks he did it for money, for flash, for…I don't know…kicks."

Jack had enough sense not to tell her that her dad was wrong. Her grandfather didn't strike him as a risk-taker or thrill-seeker. Jack knew fear when he saw it. Fear and tension together created reactions like the old man's. "No." He spoke a little sharply.

She lifted her head. "You think Grandpa Connor had some other motive? We can't know, can we?"

It was hard not to take hold of her hands, but if he did, he'd forget the team, forget the risk to her. He thought they were safe for the moment with the guys on duty. He tried to blank out the welter of voices and movement in the food court around them. A referee would be handy, a guy in a striped uniform to blow his whistle and freeze the motion, stop the noise. Jack reached for Soldier and settled for saying the key thing. "Triggers work by fear. Your grandpa's afraid."

"Now? So many years later?"

"The stroke, probably. Pathways in the brain get crossed up."

She bowed her head again.

Soldier shook himself, and Jack checked on his team's positions. He saw nothing out of the ordinary. Everyone was holding steady. "The worst fear is that the bad guys will hurt people you…love."

The word made her look up, her gaze searching his face. He was grateful for the dark glasses. He could never be sure anymore about the flow of his words. Sometimes he spoke too openly, so he kept speech to a minimum. That was part of the change in him, one his doctors had not entirely figured out in spite of the many images of his brain they'd ordered.

"You think he did it to protect us, the family?"

"Very likely." Jack could easily imagine how a man who cared about his family could be worked on by thugs like the ones who'd controlled the former owner of his house.

"I'd like to believe that, but you want to know someone completely, not just halfway." Her voice was wistful.

"He can be both, can't he? Your Santa, and a…man who did a wrong?"

She studied Jack again, as if she caught something of his own story in the question. He didn't know what she saw. Too much? His vulnerabilities, how her answer mattered, how he wanted to touch her? Or too little, just a weird guy in dark glasses?

"I don't know if I can see him again. I usually go…" A new bleaker note came into her voice. He guessed that the longing for her old connection with her grandpa was at odds with the truth that now repulsed her.

"I can find out why. The FBI…" He knew as soon as he said it that the offer was a blunder. She didn't want his interference in her family's affairs.

She shook her head. "No. No more investigating my family. I have to figure this out."

Her answer sounded like the end of the conversation. He focused his gaze on the bobbing head of the turkey, trying to think of something more to say, something that would keep her at the table, talking with him, looking at him, near him. "Did I pass your mall test?"

"I didn't mean to make it a test, exactly. I wanted to give you an exit strategy."

"I don't want to exit."

"You should." Her tone was resolute. "I've been thinking. We're not a good match." She paused again. "What's your plan for Thanksgiving?"

"Thanksgiving?"

"This Thursday when people all over America connect with their families and friends, watch parades and football, and eat themselves into food comas."

"This is another test."

She grinned. "You look seasick."

"Trying not to puke does that."

She reached for him and stopped short of touching. "Can you take anything? Peppermint tea? Papaya smoothie?"

He shuddered. "Do you need to eat?"

She shook her head. "I'll take something back to my office later, but look at us. I eat; you don't. I have possessions; you don't. I have family and friends; you don't even like people."

"I like you."

"Yes, but we shouldn't plunge ahead with this…."

"You want to go slow."

"I don't think we should go at all."

"You want me to walk away." He didn't know how he got the words out of his tight throat.

Her gaze snapped back to him, seeming to implore him to understand. "Oh, I don't know what I want. This whole thing feels like a…I don't know." She took a slow, deep breath. "One afternoon when I was ten—I think it was the first day of summer vacation—I went up the steepest hill in our neighborhood on my bike, one of those kid bikes with high handlebars, but low to the ground. The morning fog was burning off, and from the top, I could see the big refinery and the whole harbor. I took off down that hill to see how fast I could go. The bike pedals went crazy. I couldn't move my feet quick enough or get them out of the way."

She shuddered, and he waited. "What happened?"

"The back of the bike came up, and I flew off over the front. I was lucky. I rolled and lost a patch of hair from the top of my head, and had the wind knocked out of me. Lots of scrapes but no broken bones. A neighbor came out of her house and pulled me out of the street before I got run over."

He had no trouble getting her meaning. "Two dates is a bike wreck?"

"That sounds silly to you, doesn't it? Taking a life lesson from a bike accident. You've had worse things happen." She gave him another questioning glance.

"Different things," he said. He wasn't going to tell her his story. His body was screaming its impatience to touch her. He'd never known wanting like this before. "I can go slow." He tried to make a joke of it. "Walk with me. You'll see. I walk like your grandpa." That was the truth.

Her eyes flashed at him, and she released a short, rueful laugh. "You do not go slow. Your speech is slow, but your mind moves at about light speed. And you—"

"*Go*." The urgent command came through in his earpiece from Rashaad, and in the same instant, Nick stood up from his bench and Bradley picked up his laptop and coffee cup. They went their separate ways, and Jack knew they would close in behind him. The key was to distance himself from Mari, fast.

Jack put his hand on Soldier's harness and rose, giving the dog the signal to lead, then they set out across the crowded food court. He didn't look back.

Chapter 7

In Jack's absence, Mari was left with a perfect view of the fish mural at the back of the poke counter draped in tinsel and red and green globes. She stared straight ahead.

He'd just walked away.

Her phone vibrated in her purse, and she dug it out and retrieved the text.

Don't move. Don't turn around. It's okay.

She stared at the message. It was not okay. Jack Ryker had invaded her life again, or his mysterious team had. They'd been talking about knowing someone wholly, or not really knowing them at all. Obviously, she had no clue about who he was. She laid the phone on the table and tried to remain calm, but she started to shake. Out of the corner of her eye, she saw Wiggs, the tall blond mall security guard. He gazed out over the food court, sucking up a blended coffee drink, apparently unaware of whatever disturbance had caused Jack to bolt.

Nothing changed around her. Moms soothed fussing babies and toddlers. Seniors in a walking group picked up water bottles and set off for a circuit of the mall. A few teens from the local high school, phones in hand, collected mobile orders from the pizza concession.

Then she heard Shanny's voice and looked up.

"Mari? You okay?" Shanny stood looking down at her. "Are you eating?"

"I was about to order."

Shanny set down her tray of Korean Ahi and green tea, pulled out Jack's abandoned chair, and sat down. "Was that the guy? Did he just dump you?"

"He was called away on business." It was an easy excuse to make. Whatever had really happened Mari needed time to think about it.

"What is his business? Did you find out?"

Mari said the first thing that came to mind. "He's in security."

"What's wrong with him? I saw the dog, the dark glasses. Is he blind?"

"No." Mari got hold of herself. Later she would face the unanswered questions Jack left in his wake. She had to change the topic. "How was Irish Music Night?"

"Perfect. My guy was there. Fletcher. Turns out his brother went to Loyola Law with my cousin Tony. We're going out Wednesday."

"Tell me all about Fletcher," Mari said. Fletcher was a safe topic. Shanny would forget about Jack, and maybe Mari could too, for a few minutes anyway.

***

In the SUV, the team ignored Jack's dry heaves, his body's effort to empty itself of nothing. Jack sat in his usual seat with Soldier's head on his knee.

Rashaad had spotted a man taking pictures of Jack from across the food court. It had happened fast, and Rashaad didn't think the guy had caught Mari's face. Evans or his proxy had been there one minute and gone the next.

Next to Jack in the middle seat, Nick was pissed and expressing himself in a variety of unmistakable terms, including his favorite term for Jack. "You're a hemorrhoid, man."

From the shotgun seat, Bradley offered his opinion that there might be mall security footage. He was already working on getting access to it. Earlier from the parked SUV, Miguel had taken footage of everyone leaving by the mall's back exit from the instant the "go" signal came. They might get lucky.

"It means," Marcus said from the rear seat, "that Evans is here. He's watching, and he's desperate enough to risk a public appearance."

"It means," said Nick, "civilians are at risk, moms, kids, babies. Did you see that crowd?"

"Dial it back, Nick," said Rashaad. "Evans wants Jack dead. No fuss. No mess. He wants Jack to die so quietly that even Jack won't know he's been killed until Evans removes the knife from between his ribs."

"Well," said Nick. "If he stares at that woman like he did today, he'll never know what hit him."

Jack had to agree.

***

Late Tuesday night in the mall community room, the Santa-pageant performers milled about, packing up their props and costumes after a successful rehearsal. In half an hour max, Mari could go home. She kept a tight smile in place. She recognized the symptoms of a mild case of the breakup blues. The trouble with intense attraction, like the attraction she felt for Jack Ryker, was that it was exhilarating, like a wild ride, and just as likely to be brief and disastrous. She'd told him that with her bike ride story. Her throat ached, but that was from hours of trying to speak above the happy bustle around her. Telling Jack they should have ended their relationship before it went anywhere was a smart move. She should have felt wise and strong for exercising common sense, not let down and out of place in the midst of the general joy around her.

In the far corner, a lone girl elf, who had apparently missed the memo about Santa being a bringer of joy and hope, sobbed quietly next to the curtained dressing alcove, ignoring the tissue box on a table strewn with makeup containers. Suddenly, joining the elf for a good cry seemed like the perfect way to end the day.

Mari was halfway to the crying elf when a man she hadn't noticed earlier reached the girl first. Under thirty and dazzlingly good-looking in an old-school preppy way, from his blond hair to his sockless feet in expensive loafers, the man dropped to his haunches in front of the girl, slid her a box of tissues, and engaged her in conversation.

Mari couldn't hear them over the echoing chatter in the high-ceilinged community room. A few performers, including a Santa, a pair of toy soldiers, and four elves, remained in costume, listening to Ron, the sharp-voiced photographer, give directions for the last photo shoot of the night. People called to her as she passed, but Mari kept moving.

When she reached the corner, the blond man came to his feet and turned her way. His golden good looks momentarily distracted her, though he seemed not to notice.

"Mari Lynch?" He smiled.

She nodded. "Do I know you?"

"I'm Huntington, Josh Huntington, from the South Bay Neighborhood Center. We talked about Santas last week."

"Oh, hello. Yes, thank you for recommending Jorge." She turned to the huddled elf. "What's going on? Can I help?"

The girl lifted a round, tear-streaked face to Mari. She was probably sixteen and plumply pretty in an unsophisticated way, her dark eyes rimmed with smudged mascara.

"I had to use the bathroom," she said. "The photographer said I missed my chance, that I belonged with the other Santa, not this one."

Mari and Huntington exchanged a look over the girl's head. It was the sort of comment that could be mistaken for mere impatience from an adult who had been working long hours with squirrelly teenagers, but it sounded like something uglier, like a dismissal of the only plump, brown girl among the whiter elves.

"Elena's a volunteer at the center, a model to the younger kids," Huntington said. It was a statement of fact, but also a quiet challenge.

Mari glanced back at the photo shoot in progress. "We'll get you into the picture, Elena. Take a minute to check your hair and makeup and meet me by the photo backdrop."

With a grin at Huntington, the girl scampered off.

Mari turned and headed for the temporary North Pole backdrop they were using for the photo shoot. Huntington followed. He stood off to one side while she explained to Ron that whatever his ideas about the perfect promo shot, Elena belonged in it. Ron claimed he could take no responsibility if mall executives did not like the results. The conversation required Mari to use the word "nevertheless" several times and to explain the concept of welcoming everyone into the group.

When Elena returned, Ron's assistant directed her to a spot between the toy soldiers.

Through it all, Mari was conscious of Huntington studying her with an amused scrutiny.

"Thanks," he said.

"Of course." She gave him a puzzled look. "You didn't show up at our Santa rehearsal just to rescue a distressed damsel, did you?"

He laughed. "I'm the ride home for a few of the kids, but full disclosure, I was curious. Jack Ryker's a friend of mine."

Mari tried not to gape. "You? You're one of his two friends?"

"Two?" He laughed. "I guess that's about right. We went to Canyon together."

Mari could easily believe that Huntington with his effortless charm had gone to a posh private boys school. "He…Jack…told me he had three friends, counting the dog."

"Ah," he said. "Ryker's a bit of a Grinch, but his permafrost is thawing. I did some work for him this summer, helping him launch his philanthropy."

"Philanthropy?" Her voice sounded incredulous in her own ears.

"Hard to believe, I know. He works with brain-injured veterans."

Mari wanted to hear more, which was nuts. Anything she learned about Jack now would be like a postmortem report on their nonstarter relationship. She focused on the group in front of the camera. The elves and Santa struck different poses as the camera clicked and flashed. Elena beamed happily from between the toy soldiers, looking adorable, the tears of a few minutes before gone. Mari wished she could banish her own foolish blues as easily.

She turned to Huntington. Maybe he knew something that would help her make sense of what happened at lunch. If she understood, she wouldn't feel dumb, wouldn't feel that nagging sense of having made a mistake. "Jack's not a vet, but did—"

"…something happen to him? You mean the chair, the dog, his speech? He was injured in Afghanistan. He's not up-front about it."

"*Up-front*? He's not up-front about anything. He's a controlling recluse with serious trust issues."

Huntington grinned at her outburst. "That sums it up. Our other friend, Sloan, calls Ryker a locked bank vault." Huntington glanced at Elena, gave the girl a thumbs-up sign, and turned back to Mari. "I thought maybe he'd open up to a…woman, to *you*, actually. Tell you about this thing he's doing for vets with the video game that retrains the brain."

"Sorry. Not going to happen. He ended our…connection today. He walked away."

"You're kidding, right? He'd never do that. He…"

Mari had to get a grip. She was babbling to a stranger, a clever stranger, who knew how to rouse her curiosity about Jack with his talk of philanthropy. "Why am I telling you this? I don't even know you."

"Right. Sorry." Huntington offered Mari a rueful grin. "It's just that Ryker has a pretty big crush on you, and he could use someone in his corner."

"Besides his crew of supersized bodyguards?"

"I don't think he wants to sleep with any of them." Huntington spoke in a low, dry voice for her alone, and Mari heard every word.

The photo shoot ended. The photographer's assistant started breaking down the lighting and screens. Santa and his elves fanned out, removing hats, heading for the curtained alcove to change. A glowing Elena came their way. She thanked Mari, eyes bright, a happy flush in her cheeks. Huntington reminded her that it was late, and she hurried off. Three other teenagers waited nearby, bent over their phones, texting.

"Look," Huntington said to Mari. "I apologize. I've been way out of line here." He laughed. "I owe Ryker a lot, and I had some luck matchmaking for our friend Sloan. I guess I got carried away."

The word *matchmaking* surprised her. Huntington wanted Jack and Mari to get together?

Huntington did contrition well, and she imagined that with his eye-candy good looks, women generally forgave him almost anything, but she couldn't reply. She was stuck on the idea that Jack wanted to sleep with her. She'd sensed that he was strongly attracted to her, but could not understand why. He was nothing like the men who responded to her online dating profile.

"Thanks again," Huntington said. "For taking on Jorge and looking out for Elena. I know a six-year-old boy who can't wait to meet Santa this year. See you later."

Mari mumbled something, but she hardly knew what. *What could a man like Huntington possibly owe Jack Ryker?*

Elena returned with a backpack over her shoulder. The other teens collected their belongings, and Huntington led them all away.

Santiago, the head of the night cleaning crew, waved to Mari as his team arrived. Mari waved back. She could go home.

Chapter 8

Late Thanksgiving night, Jack sat in the chair in his bare living room, thinking about a steep downhill bike ride and the woman who'd once taken it. Above the Strand, the evening blackness stretched to distant lights winking on the Palos Verdes hill and on boats heading north to the marina. The steady, silent darkness of the living room meant that Jack didn't need his dark glasses.

At peace after a restless day lifting his nose to catch the smell of roasting turkey, Soldier lay on the floor, beside Jack. The dog had settled only when Rashaad treated him to some leftovers.

Jack had turned down invites from Sloan to meet at his mother's house in Redondo Beach and from Huntington to join him and Emma and Emma's young son Max at Emma's grandparents' house in Beverly Hills. Having his friends look out for him was a new thing. He couldn't remember a time since he'd left home at seventeen when he had been invited to a family gathering. Huntington's invite ended with a line of text Jack couldn't get out of his head.

FYI. She thinks you ended it.

For two days, Huntington's message had distracted him, interfering with his concentration as Cole pushed him through hard workouts and as he studied still shots from the mall security footage Bradley had acquired. Jack needed to focus. He owed it to his team to keep the mission front and center in his mind. And he owed it to Mari not to involve her.

Evans being at the mall meant two things: one, Evans was nearby watching Jack's house, and two, Evans was waiting for an opportunity to get at Jack away from the house. Any way Jack looked at it, he remained trapped. Evans wanted a crowd, and Jack had a lot of thinking to do to turn the tables and trap Evans without anyone else getting hurt. They had been prepared and lucky in the spring when Evans sent a lone gunman to the concert that launched their cross-platform video game. Jack didn't want to depend on luck. And he didn't want to think about Evans.

Persistent, unsatisfied sexual desire had uncomfortable ways of making itself known. It had been a constant joke in high school, especially in study hall where the big dictionaries were kept. He and every other Canyon boy had searched those dictionaries for words about sex. He had scored big laughs for his find—*priapism*. He had a long non-history with women, and he knew why. In high school, he'd learned to hate the jokes and the lies men in power, like his father and Headmaster Chambers, told themselves about how women wanted sex. He had vowed never to be one of those men. Consulting for clients who were buying or selling arms, he'd often encountered powerful men who offered the services of women as a perk of doing business. He'd always declined. Someone's sister or daughter was not a thing to be served up with the amenities of luxury hotel rooms, private planes, and island retreats.

Falling for Mari Lynch was a first for him, like going back to the beginning and starting over with a clean slate. Only the attraction between them clearly scared her off, or maybe Jack had with his disappearing act. That was the point of Huntington's message. Subtle bastard that he was, Huntington wanted Jack to see things from Mari's point of view.

Jack was trying to work out in his mind how to keep from scaring her when Soldier stirred and came to his feet. Bradley was in the hall, talking, his low voice answered by a softer, higher-pitched one. The door opened, admitting a stabbing shaft of light, and the visitor entered. The door closed. Darkness swallowed up whoever it was, but Jack knew.

"It's me," Mari said. "I can't see a thing."

Jack's eyes adjusted instantly, but his heart rate kicked up. He didn't know how she'd approached the house, but if she'd come from the Strand and turned up the walk street, her entry into the house could only be seen from the alley his guys controlled.

"Don't move," he said. He levered himself up out of the chair. Soldier stood, alert, ready for any command. Jack sent him to guard the door.

He stepped between her and the windows behind him. He didn't think Evans had night vision equipment that could penetrate the house's defenses, but now that he knew Evans was out there somewhere, he would take no chances on Evans catching a glimpse of her through the windows.

Light from the Strand and a sliver from a crack at the base of the door let Jack see her. She stood a few feet from the door, wearing a coat and holding a container. A dizzying montage of images flashed in his head of taking her in his arms, kissing her, and falling with her in a tangle of limbs onto the sofa in the corner. His old self could have made those moves. Not now. He waited for the crazy tumult of his body's desire to slow down.

"Take a minute," he said. She moved slightly. "See me?"

"Yes."

He took a couple of surprisingly steady steps toward her. "What have you got?"

"My mom's whipped sweet potatoes. Butter, brown sugar, and pecans. Not to be missed."

He stopped near enough to reach out to her. She thrust the container forward, and the sweet, homey smell reached him. His warm fingers closed over her cold ones. For a moment he couldn't move, couldn't break the contact.

"Thank you," he said. He backed up and put the container down on the seat of his chair. He wasn't going to sit in it if he could help it. "Will you stay?" he asked.

"For a while."

He came back to her and took her hand, holding it, cold and trembling, in his. He tugged, and she yielded to his pull. "Feel brave enough to sit on the sofa?"

She gave a shaky laugh. "No sex."

"No bike ride down a steep hill."

"Is that what you thought the story meant?" she asked. "That I didn't want sex?"

They reached the edge of the sofa. "Do you need your coat?"

"No." She pulled free of his hand and worked the buttons. The coat slipped from her shoulders with a silky rustle that sent sizzling messages straight to his groin. He caught the coat and tossed it across the short end of the sofa. He was glad Cole had made him practice getting on and off the thing. It had been part of his early workouts. He arranged himself in the corner of the L, his legs down the long side, his arms along the cushion backs, making room for her. He didn't know why she'd come. He couldn't be sure she'd stay. She stood a moment longer, maybe calculating the risk. Then she sat and scooted next to him.

Her arm came against his side. The sofa cushion dipped slightly where her hip touched his, and the fabric of her skirt floated down across his shin. The scent of her filled his head, clean and delicate, fresh like air after rain. A different dizziness, not the usual vertigo of sudden movement, overcame him. His stomach did some kind of flip he didn't know an internal organ could do.

"What were you doing that I interrupted just now?" she asked.

"Thinking." He swallowed. "Did you visit your grandpa?"

"I wanted to, but my cousin, who cares for him, said he was too agitated today. Did you investigate him further?"

"I can. The FBI has a thick file on the lawyer who owned this house."

"You're not FBI?"

"No."

"What then?"

He didn't answer. He didn't know how to tell her who he was. He was a guy who had screwed up big time, a guy once so detached from others, he thought his actions touched no one. Now he was a man with a team and a mission. They had an FBI contact, an agent of the Fugitive Task Force from the LA field office. Agent Arias had worked a case where some guy set up a phony company and scammed the government out of millions on no-bid security contracts after the Snowden leaks. That was how Evans operated, but Evans sold his wares to an enemy, and marines had died.

Jack didn't know how long he'd been lost in his thoughts. She twisted next to him and pressed her fingers to his lips. His mouth went dry. He couldn't speak if he tried. Her touch, spontaneous and voluntary, woke a sense he did not know he had, one he had not trained to control—awareness. For a moment it overpowered his other senses, and the jarring confusion among them went away. There was only Mari.

"You don't have to reveal your top-level security clearance or make some dreadful confession," she said. "Try something easier. Tell me what you were thinking about tonight, sitting here in the dark. Alone."

He rejected total honesty. "A Christmas tree and lights."

"Really?"

"Surprised?"

"Very. Can you explain anything?"

"About…what happened Monday?" He couldn't. He saw that plainly. Already he might have involved her in a risk he didn't want to contemplate. He hadn't expected her to come to him, and he'd thought that by avoiding communication, he was protecting her from Evans's notice.

"Can you tell me about the chair, the darkness?"

That he could manage. "The chair works like a carpenter's level. There are some loose bits in my inner ear that throw off my balance. The chair seat adjusts to make sure the loose bits stay in the bubble."

"And the darkness?"

"Most artificial light is not steady. The dark glasses reduce the flicker."

"The mall must have been a sensory nightmare."

He had no intention of telling her about the cold sweats or the nausea. "Tell me something. Why did you come tonight?"

It was her turn to fall silent. He could sense her figuring out what she wanted to say. He didn't know what he hoped. He lifted his arm from the back of the sofa and took her hand in his, resting their joined palms against his thigh. It was a bold move, but she didn't resist.

"Something draws me to you. Well." She laughed. "Something besides the obvious. I'm trying to understand it. And I want a 'do-over,' even if we still don't…work."

"Because of Huntington?" He had to ask.

He felt the little shake of her head. "Something he said got me thinking. But mainly because of you. You aren't like ordinary men, you know."

That didn't sound good, but he had to ask. "I'm not?"

"Well, for one, you're not watching a Thanksgiving football game with a beer in one hand, yelling madly at the TV as a herd of behemoths pushes an odd-shaped ball back and forth on a patch of artificial turf."

"Right." He didn't think she minded that difference too much.

"And for two, I can't imagine bringing you home to my family. There are expectations, you see." She sighed.

He didn't see. No woman had brought him to meet her family.

"I think you'd bolt when Mom put garlic mashed potatoes on the table. Or when Uncle Larry told a loud joke and everyone snorted with laughter." She squeezed his hand as she spoke. He didn't despair, but she was right that meeting her family would be a challenge for him.

"You brought other…dates home? Non-bolting dates."

He had to wait an interminable time for an answer.

"You should know. There was someone in my life for two years. Until last January, I lived with him in a condo in the marina."

It was a rushed little confession. And she left out how it ended. He wanted to know more. He wanted to find the guy and maybe rearrange the architecture of his nose.

"And you?"

"No one in the last two years," he said.

She slipped her hand from his and twisted toward him, sitting up away from the sofa back. Her knee brushed his thigh, causing his brain to shut down briefly as sensation overwhelmed him. "That," she said, tapping him on the chest, "is so you. Honest and utterly…uninformative."

She swung around, lowering her feet to the floor.

"Wait." He'd missed some clue. There was something he should have said.

"I have to go now, but I'm not walking out on us. We're not done." She stood and snatched up her coat. Soldier stirred at the door.

"I'll see you again?" He sounded pathetic. He hadn't been pathetic in a mud cell with guys beating him. "I know places we can meet in daylight. Private places." He had to slow her down, borrow time to get off the sofa.

She shrugged into her coat. "Alone? Or with your…guards?"

He managed to get to his feet. "Security matters. Bradley will get you home tonight."

"I'm working. I have to go to the mall."

"Bradley will get you there." Jack wasn't going to back down on that point. Bradley could get her out of the house without anyone seeing her or seeing where she went.

"Fine." She didn't look at him as she spoke.

He took her by the shoulders and turned her around. “Mari.” Her name came out in a voice he barely recognized as his. “You asked me what I was thinking about tonight.”

She tilted her face up to his, her eyes big and dark with the question.

“This,” he said. He leaned forward and kissed her, and everything went still, her mouth soft and smooth under his, open in surprise. His heart paused, waiting long milliseconds to beat again. Then she kissed him back, leaning in, hanging on, her hands gripping his shirt, bunching the wool over his ribs. The box at his waist shifted, alerting his team.

The door opened. Light spilled in, and they broke apart. She stepped into the hall and spoke to Bradley in a cheerful, unaffected voice. The door closed, and Jack was alone again in the dark with the dog—and hope.

Chapter 9

The interior of the luxury black SUV was cold and tomblike, silent except for the rumble of the engine. Mari's cheerful "Merry Christmas" as she climbed in received no answer from Jack. He sat, apparently frozen, belted into a seat next to his chair, which was secured to the floor by metal rails. She caught her toe on one of them as she squeezed around him into a seat.

The automatic door closed behind her, and she surrendered her purse to Bradley, Jack's ever-present security guard, who hopped into the front passenger seat. He put her purse on the console between the front seats. The strap dangled her way, and she figured she could reach it if she had to, and buckled her seat belt. The silent driver pulled the SUV away from the curb at the mall's north entrance. They were heading for Mari's favorite family-run tree lot to pick a tree for Jack's living room. They'd made the date in a brief exchange of texts, but now it didn't feel like a date. It felt like a mash-up between a tense family argument and a special ops mission. She did not yet understand his need for bodyguards. Though LA had agencies that offered such services to high-net-worth individuals, Jack seemed to have his own people, not hired professionals.

She tried to assess the mood in the car. Jack had retreated somewhere inside himself, beside her, but not looking her way, his profile stony. It was the first time she'd ridden with him. She wondered if his silence had to do with the constraints of his situation, not driving, having the chair parked next to him. He'd confessed his balance problem to her, so she wondered if the car's motion bothered him.

She wanted to nudge him, to remind him that he'd kissed her. She'd been thinking happy thoughts about that kiss for two days, but she couldn't feel any connection between them. They were strangers again.

She checked on her purse—still there—and turned to the window. Outside the darkened glass the streets were a faint blur of Christmas lights as they passed. In her family, the tree-picking expedition had always been a raucous, laughter-filled adventure. They'd go at night, jammed into the car singing "Jingle Bells" and "Rudolph," and oohing and aahing over light displays, while her parents negotiated over whether it was to be a noble fir or a Scotch pine year. Every year her mom argued for a noble with its open-branch pattern where ornaments hung freely. Her dad countered with the smell and the practical water-retention qualities of the Scotch pine. The argument would be resolved over hot cider in Christmas mugs at the tree lot. Picking a Christmas tree was supposed to be fun.

She turned to Jack. She needed to change the mood in the SUV. "I fired Santa today," she said.

He gave a slight start and flicked a glance at her.

At least he heard her. She waited.

"Why?"

"This particular Santa didn't like being sneezed on or having his beard pulled or getting all hot in his red suit." She sighed. "It turns out he didn't like parents, or their kids. I was so *wrong* about him. He wasn't good at sitting in a chair for six hours."

That made him turn more fully toward her and stare. She knew he read the challenge in her words, and she realized abruptly how rare it was for him to turn his head.

Her phone rang, and she lunged for her purse and snagged it, pulling it into her lap and fishing for her phone. It could only be Abby.

Bradley turned in the front seat. "Ryker," he snapped.

Mari turned the phone over in her palm. Abby's name flashed on the screen, and Mari started to swipe when Jack grabbed her wrist.

"Don't answer," he said.

Mari held on in spite of the hard grip. "It's my cousin. She only calls if something's wrong with my grandpa."

"Give the phone back to Bradley."

Mari stared at him. He really was a stranger, and for the first time, she thought him a scary stranger. Her heart raced. She was in a car with three men she really didn't know at all. She made herself speak slowly and clearly. "My cousin needs my help with Grandpa."

The brutal grip didn't relax. With his other hand, Jack pried the phone from her fingers and gave it to Bradley, who shut it down and turned away.

"Security protocol, Ms. Lynch," said Bradley.

Jack released her wrist, and she shifted as far from him as the seat belt permitted. "Take me back to the mall," she said. Her voice shook. "We're done."

He didn't answer, didn't look at her, so she huddled next to the window, hugging her arms to her body, her throat aching. She expected the driver to turn them around, but he neither slowed nor changed direction. Abruptly a light switched on next to her, and Jack passed Bradley a tablet, its screen bright with a map grid.

"You sure?" Bradley asked.

"Yes."

The driver changed course, and they sped, the only word for it, along a residential street that undulated across the ridge of dunes marking the eastern edge of the South Bay beach cities. Mari lost all sense of where they were. "Where are you taking me?" she asked Jack's rigid profile.

She thought he'd never answer. The car didn't slow. The driver apparently had an aversion to braking until he didn't. The car made a sharp turn and came to a crawl.

"Your grandpa's house," Jack said.

"What?" She wanted to hit him.

"You said your grandpa needed…"

The car pulled up to a curb. Bradley hopped out, and then the SUV door opened at the curb in front of her grandpa's modest bungalow.

"Go," Jack said.

Mari unbuckled her seat belt and scrambled out of the car. A stiff cold breeze blew as Abby sat on the top of the low brick steps at the courtyard entry. Light spilled from the open gate behind her, and she looked up as Mari approached. "Don't you answer your phone?" she shouted. "I've been calling for twenty minutes."

"Don't have my phone. Tell me what happened."

Abby looked past Mari, her eyes widening. Mari glanced over her shoulder at Jack and Soldier, now standing on the sidewalk.

"Are they police?" Abby came to her feet.

"Police? Just…friends. Tell me what's going on with Grandpa."

"He's gone."

"Gone?" Mari's knees gave a little, and her heart caught in her chest.

"Missing," Abby clarified.

Mari's heart resumed beating. "Did you call the police?"

"Not yet. Don't blame me. He was awful today. In the morning, he wouldn't put on his shoes. We went through every pair. He just kept shouting, 'Wrong, wrong.' I had to let him go barefoot. After lunch, he tore apart his closet. His room is a disaster. I put him in the den just for a minute, so I could make dinner." Abby shivered. She had clearly been out in the wind too long. "And then he was gone. I called you."

"I'm sorry. I'm not blaming you." Mari heard the pain and frustration in Abby's voice, but the main thing was to find her grandfather. "So, Grandpa's barefoot and wearing what?"

"A red shirt, I think."

"Okay. You stay here in case he comes back. I'll look for him, ask the neighbors if anyone's seen him. If we have to, we call the police. Right?"

"Right. Wait. How will I reach you?"

"Don't worry. I'll check with you." She would once she got her phone back. "Go inside. Get warm."

As soon as Abby turned away, Mari strode up to Jack. She needed her phone, and she needed him and his wire-wearing security guards gone.

"My grandpa has wandered off," she said. "He's old, frail, and not able to communicate well. He could fall or wander into traffic or…"

"I heard."

She held out her hand. "I'd like my phone. I'm going to look for him."

"Bradley will contact your cousin. The guys will do a perimeter sweep. They know what your grandpa looks like. I'm with you."

"Without your…team?"

Jack touched the black box at his waist. "They can find me."

The SUV pulled away.

Mari stared at him. "You. I'm so angry with you I—"

She spun and stalked for the corner, refusing to slow down. Let Jack keep up if he could. He had the dog and a phone. Her grandpa was out there somewhere, lost, driven by the confusion in his mind and some sense of urgency.

At the corner, she peered into the dark, trying to think what would influence the direction a confused old man would take. North, she hoped, away from the little strip mall that fronted the Coast Highway, but she didn't want to think what could happen to him if she was wrong.

"I know this neighborhood." Jack's voice came from beside her. He and Soldier had caught up. "He'll go toward lights." He pointed to a house two doors down on their right, where a low white fence along the front of the property was draped with icicle lights. In the little yard, a family of plastic blow-up reindeer grazed.

Mari clenched her jaw. She wouldn't give him the satisfaction of knowing he was helpful. He was a controlling weirdo, so far from ordinary, he might as well be extraterrestrial.

She went to the door of the house and knocked. A curtain twitched in a window next to the door, but no one answered. She marched to the next lighted house, and the next. Each time, whoever answered glanced suspiciously at Jack and Soldier and shook their heads. No one had seen Connor Lynch.

"You're not helping, you know," she told him when her next knock went unanswered. "You scare people, people who probably know my grandpa. He's lived here for nearly fifteen years."

He pointed to a realtor's sign in the yard. "They could be new."

At the seventh house they tried, the woman who answered the door knew Mari's grandpa. "Oh, honey, I'm so sorry," she said. "I haven't seen him tonight, but try Hillcrest, the cul-de-sac. It slopes slightly downhill, and my mom used to end up there when she went walking."

Mari thanked her. "Abby never takes him there," she told Jack.

"Try it," he said.

Hillcrest Drive hooked like a hockey stick. The straight upper section was dark without any Christmas displays, but where the street bent up slightly toward one end, palm tree trunks wore white collars of lights, and red and green lights twinkled and blinked, outlining the shapes of roofs and trees. Music played. Reindeer pranced on rooftops. Snowmen and polar bears waved from front porches.

Mari glanced back. Jack had stopped several yards behind her, standing still with Soldier against his leg, bracing him. He pulled a pair of dark glasses from his board shirt pocket and put them on. They'd walked near a mile. She didn't know how he was managing it. She didn't care.

Somewhere ahead of them, a dog barked from behind the side gate of a brightly lit house near the closed end of the street. A huge black truck sat in the driveway, and seated by the front door was a white-haired man in a red plaid shirt. Mari hurried forward.

On a little slab of concrete that could hardly be called a porch, her grandpa sat in a woven patio chair. Next to him stood a side table with a plate of cookies and a glass of milk. His feet were immersed in an orange plastic tub. A petite, dark-haired woman of perhaps fifty stood beside him. She wore a bright red T-shirt and a Santa hat with a blue beach towel draped over her shoulder. The copper tea kettle in her hand released a thin wisp of steam.

"Did you come to see Santa?" she asked Mari.

Mari nodded but couldn't speak.

"I'm Mae," said the woman. "Santa lost his boots on this trip. We're warming his feet up in a bath."

Mari took the stone path to the little porch. Her grandpa's red and black buffalo plaid shirt was mis-buttoned over his lean frame. His white hair stuck out in wild clumps. Suddenly, his wrong shoes, his torn apart closet, and his wandering made sense. He was a Saturday Santa, and it was a Christmas season Saturday.

She stepped up onto the porch. "Hi, Grandpa," she said. "It's me, Mari." She took his hand. For a moment she thought he wouldn't know her; then his gaze met hers, and his eyes seemed to focus.

"The kids couldn't find me, sweetheart," he said with a shake of his head.

Mari squeezed his hand. "I did, Grandpa," she said. She turned to thank Mae, but Mae was looking at Jack standing on the sidewalk at the end of the path.

"Jack." Mae smiled warmly at him. "Hello. We missed you at Thanksgiving."

"Hi, Mae," he said. "Is Sloan here?"

"Just his truck. I'm borrowing it to get a tree."

Mari held her grandpa's hand as Mae went up to Jack, kissed him on the cheek, and slipped her arm through his with easy affection. Mari didn't know what was more astonishing—that Jack knew her grandfather's kind neighbor, or that the woman touched him freely as if he were not as prickly as the spiniest urchin in the sea.

"Can you come in?" Mae asked him.

Jack removed the dark glasses. His gaze met Mari's, and she gave a tiny shake of her head. She thought she could bring herself to thank him for helping her find Grandpa Connor, but she was too angry to forgive him for scaring her or for being a controlling jerk.

Behind Jack, the black SUV pulled into the cul-de-sac, circled, and parked at the curb. Mae gave the car a brief glance, slipped out of Jack's arm, and returned to the porch.

"I'll sit with your grandpa," she told Mari. "If you need to say good night."

Mari strode down the walk and stopped six feet from Jack. He looked beautiful and baffled. The breeze had brushed the dark hair back from his forehead. His brows met in a pucker above eyes full of puzzlement and loss, as if he had no idea how their date had gone so wrong. Mari steeled herself against a warm rush of sympathy. She owed him politeness, nothing more.

"I messaged Bradley. Your cousin knows you found your grandpa," he said.

"Thank you, and thank you for your help in the search. I can manage from here if you will return my phone and my purse."

She thought he would protest or insist on taking her home, but he merely touched some hidden spot at his waist. The SUV's doors opened, and Bradley emerged. He brought Mari her purse and phone, and she took them and backed away. Bradley stepped between her and Jack in a protective move, as if she were a threat to Jack instead of the other way around, so she turned to her grandpa. His head had slumped down on his chest. She quickened her steps.

On the porch, Mae bent down, dipped a hand into the water around Grandpa Connor's feet, then added more from her kettle. She looked up at Mari and lifted a finger to her lips. "He's asleep. I brought you a chair."

Mari took the offered chair. When she looked up, the SUV was gone. "I can't thank you enough. We were so worried."

"I can imagine. I take it that he used to play Santa somewhere."

"At the Coast Plaza Mall, always on a Saturday. I thought he'd forgotten everything with some recent strokes he's had, but apparently memories resurface."

Mae settled on the porch step. "I'm Mae Sloan, by the way. My son Will and your…friend Jack Joyce went to school together."

"Joyce?"

"Sorry, I forgot. He's changed his name, hasn't he? The boys, *men* now, I have to remind myself, have been working together this year to save their old school from scandal and financial shenanigans on the part of the former headmaster."

Mari hardly knew what to say. Her feelings about Jack…Joyce…Ryker, whoever he really was, seesawed wildly from one moment to the next. "Jack told me he had two school friends."

"He has no family left, so we try to coax him into ours, but he's a bit—"

"Feral?" The word slipped out.

Mae laughed. "Yes, I think that's it. He's wary of affection and love. He's been out in the cold so long."

Mari kept silent. Somewhere the romance gods were laughing at her. Every time Jack did something outrageous, like taking charge, like scaring her witless, a friend of his appeared to defend him. What Mari needed to do was forget Jack and get Grandpa Connor home.

"Mae, do you mind staying with my grandpa while I call my cousin Abby, his caregiver?"

"Not at all."

In a few moments it was settled. Abby would bring her car round to Mae's, and together she and Mari would get Grandpa back home and settled.

In no time, Abby pulled up in front of Mae's house. At the sound of Abby's voice, Grandpa Connor gave a little start, lifted his head, and looked around, his brow furrowed in bafflement. Mari took his hand again. "Hi, Grandpa, it's Mari. You've finished your Santa shift. Can we give you a lift home?"

For a moment, she thought he might refuse, but with Mae's help, they toweled his feet dry and helped him put on the boat shoes that Abby had brought for him. Between them, Abby and Mari got him into Abby's car. At the curb, Mari thanked Mae again and got a quick hug in return. There was more to say, but first Mari and Abby needed to get their grandpa home safe and sound.

"Merry Christmas, Santa." Mae waved to Grandpa Connor as they pulled away.

Back at the bungalow, they settled him in his bed, and Abby made her position clear. "I'm not going through that again. Tomorrow we have to take some steps to secure this place."

"I know."

Abby went on listing her ideas for door locks and services that kept track of the elderly, and Mari listened, nodding when Abby pressed for agreement. She offered to talk with their neighbors and with Mae Sloan to give them a number to call if they should see Grandpa Connor wandering. Mari recognized Abby's need to do something. It was Abby's way of being worried. She gave her cousin a quick hug.

"You don't have your car, do you? How are you getting home?" Abby asked.

Mari pulled out her phone. "No problem. I'll book a ride."

"But who were those guys in the SUV? There was a wheelchair, wasn't there?"

"They were just…mall security," said Mari. "We won't see them again."

Abby looked skeptical. "Not the cute one? He looked like he might be into you."

"I don't think so." Mari was done with Jack. What she needed was a good night's sleep. Tomorrow would be a new day. She'd start looking for a real Saturday Santa.

She held on to that thought on the way home. Just at the last minute as her driver waited to make a left against oncoming traffic on the avenue, she thought she saw a black SUV parked at the entrance to her alley. When they made the turn, it was gone.

Chapter 10

Rain began to fall in the late afternoon when Jack pushed away from his computer. He maneuvered the chair to the edge of the shadows and stared out at the horizon where sky and sea fused in a silver gloom.

None of the guys had spoken to him for hours. The silence started at breakfast after Miguel invited Jack to go on thinking with that most male part of his anatomy and not his brain if he wanted to get himself killed. He didn't defend himself. They weren't wrong about his thinking, and he could take their anger.

His tree-buying date with Mari had probably been doomed before it began. In the face of the guys' disapproval and silence in the car, her cheerful greeting died on her lips. She'd offered Jack a teasing challenge with her remark about firing Santa, and he'd been trying to shift his emotional gears to answer her when her phone rang. He'd lost her at once to her family, the people she really cared about.

All day at his desk, his mind had been stuck on her, on getting her back. He was pretty sure he had done the right thing when she got the call that her grandpa was in trouble. Maybe he'd ruined another "date" between them by taking control, but he hadn't seen any other way of handling the situation. At the time what had mattered was staying with her, helping her, and he'd counted on his team to keep them both safe. She'd charged down the sidewalk, single-minded and self-forgetful, focused on finding her grandfather, oblivious of any danger to herself.

Jack had been distracted by the view of her striding ahead of him in jeans and a snowy white sweater. Her black fleece vest and red wool scarf could hardly have kept out the cold wind off the ocean. He had paid no attention to women's clothing for years. Now he found himself thinking that her clothes touched her everywhere, wondering how those clothes came off. Cole's training sessions had not included undressing a woman.

Staring at the darkening horizon, Jack tried to recall with precision her expression in that last moment before Bradley stepped between them. That was the moment that mattered. His visual memory remained unimpaired by the blow to his head that had damaged his balance. He was good at reconstructing a detailed picture of a single instant, capturing it like a screenshot.

From the curb in front of Mae's house, the scene had a few key elements: in the background Mae and Connor Lynch on the porch under a string of old-fashioned colored lights along the house eaves. In the driveway to his right Sloan's oversize black pickup truck. In the center of the scene facing him, Mari. He made himself zero in on the puzzled angle of her head, the pucker between her brows, the tentative expression in her eyes. There was some clue there that he recognized as important even if he couldn't read it clearly.

He didn't think she hated or pitied him, which was good. It was some expectation she had of him, some way he'd missed the mark. It meant that she wasn't going to come to Jack this time. But she didn't give up easily on people, flawed people. He knew that about her. Connor Lynch had disappointed her, and she hadn't abandoned him. That was the thing that gave Jack hope. As he concentrated on the scene in his head, his inner vision narrowed to the black truck in Mae Sloan's driveway. He knew what to do to get Mari speaking to him again and who could help him do it, someone inexplicably on his side: Sloan's mom, Mae.

Jack would go to Mari, and because the guys would be against his going to see her, he would have to break protocol. Big time. And he would have to do it without alerting the team. But as he analyzed the situation, he realized that he had one member of the team who would side with him unquestioningly—Soldier. With a text to Mae, with a slight bit of deception and some manipulation of Soldier's evening walk schedule, Jack, not Rashaad or Marcus, would leave the house with the dog. Each man would think the other was walking the dog.

Jack made himself picture different routes to Mari's unit at the back of a walk street house until he found a feasible one. Would it work? He thought so. He'd have Soldier with him, and the team, focused on external security threats, would not be expecting Jack's escape. Was he crazy? No question, but would he do something crazy to see her again? Yes.

***

By late afternoon Sunday, Mari had created a new Santa schedule and notified the participants. She'd spent her lunch hour at Grandpa Connor's, keeping him company and putting his closet back in order while her Uncle Dan, Abby's dad, and Abby installed locks on the doors and gate to prevent another episode of wandering.

On her way back to work, she stopped by Mae Sloan's bungalow. No one answered the door. By daylight, on a gloomy, overcast day, the neighborhood looked ordinary and dull, a place where no one ever got lost or hurt. Without a black truck in the driveway or a mysterious SUV at the curb, the quiet street inspired no worry, no adrenaline rush, no frustrating sense of loss.

A deflated feeling dogged her when she returned to her office. She checked her email one last time, then closed her laptop. She wanted to thank Mae Sloan for her kindness, and as she gathered her coat and bag, she thought of a way.

Pretty in Pots was the mall's flower shop, run by Mari's friend Rachel Benson. Rachel, like Mari and Shanny, was a fan of the mall's morning boot camp for women in retail.

The long narrow shop was lined on either side with mirrored walls above pine cabinets. The effect was like entering a fragrant grove. At Christmas, Rachel devoted one half of the shop to trees, wreaths, and garlands, and the other half to blue and white Hannukah displays. Mari paused just inside the shop to breathe in the heady scents of living greenery, cedar and fir, gardenia, tuberose, and lavender.

"Be right with you," Rachel called from her work area at the back of the store.

"Hey, Rachel, it's Mari." Mari headed through the store and poked her head into the back room. Rachel looked up from an arrangement she was making. "Oh, hi, Mari. I hear you fired Santa."

"I chose the wrong man for the job." Mari offered her friend a rueful smile.

Rachel laughed. "Oh well, you're not the first woman to do that." She stuck a white rose into a small block of green floral sponge.

"You know my mixed feelings about the jolly old elf." Rachel, whose kids were eight and ten, made her shop a yearly refuge for kids whose families didn't do Christmas. For Jewish kids, she had baskets of dreidels, and coloring and story books that told of the miraculous oil jar and burning lights. In the back of the store, she kept a supply of traditional sugary, jam-filled donuts. And she was always on the lookout for elements of other families' celebrations.

"There will be another Santa to take his place," Mari reminded her.

"Bring him on. We're ready." Rachel grinned again. "Did you want something today?"

"I want to send a thank-you arrangement to a Mae Sloan in Redondo." Mari pulled out her phone to check the address. "One of your small-vase compositions, I think."

Rachel had a way of grouping a tight mix of flowers to make a big impact. She opened a refrigerated cabinet to reveal a shelf of small seasonal bouquets. "I've got some made up if you want to take a look. Any particular reason for the thank you?"

Mari looked them over as she explained Mae's kindness to her wandering grandpa.

"Oh, Mari, I'm sorry."

"Thanks, Rachel. He's okay now. He just wanted to be Santa again."

Rachel offered a quick hug. "You know your Grandpa Connor is the one Santa I never avoid. Now what do you think of this one?" Rachel held up a mix of white and pink roses, silver eucalyptus leaves, and tiny cones.

"Perfect."

"Okay, I'm on it. Just give me a minute to finish here. You'll find paper and cards in that drawer for the address and a note."

Mari opened a drawer beneath one of Rachel's display Christmas trees, this one decorated with birds and ribbons. "You know, for a woman who doesn't do Christmas, you make beautiful trees."

"Are you putting one up this year?" Rachel knew the whole history of Mari's breakup the previous January.

Mari picked a card from the drawer and looked for a pen. Nearly a year had passed since her breakup. She'd been starry-eyed and foolish when she moved in with Grant, her ex, thinking they were on the path to happily ever after together. She was making up for that past folly now.

"You know I was okay. I was fine. This morning I went to early church. Big mistake. I realized I'm one of them—the white-haired crowd: the quiet ones who sit alone, pews apart from each other."

"What?" Rachel looked up from the arrangement she was making.

"They all know me. I'm one of them, a singleton, alone at Christmas."

"Mari, you are twenty-eight and between boyfriends, however silly a term that is. You're lucky to be free of Grant, who was the king of self-absorption. Go home and put up a tree. You love Christmas."

"I have to face the ornament box first."

Rachel laughed. "A good first step. I'm sure there's a law that says *Don't put old ornaments on a new tree*, or something. Besides, I thought Shanny said you had a new man in your life."

Mari sighed. "Actually, I fired him too."

"Wow, you are having a day. Let me take care of the thank-you bouquet. You go home and make a cup of tea or pour a glass of wine and weed out those old ornaments. Bring them to me if you like. And I'll save you a donut."

"Thanks, Rachel."

***

By nine, the afternoon's drizzle had become steady rain, and Mari slid open the door of her narrow balcony above the alley, letting in the swish and patter of it. She had fortified herself to face the ornament box with a cup of tea, and put on her favorite flannel PJ bottoms and a red T-shirt. She cranked up a playlist of old-fashioned carols, dragged the ornament box down from the top of her closet, and went to work, purging the collection from the "Grant" era.

She'd separated the ornaments into two piles on the table in the dining area off her open kitchen, and she had to laugh at the stark contrast between them. Clearly, she and Grant had not been meant for each other after all. The ornaments they'd acquired together mostly came from his mother: fragile, exquisite things that Mari suspected were an attempt to correct her taste for rustic, folk-art pieces and family memorabilia. Her pile included rough wooden angels, felt birds and woolly sheep, and hand-painted Santas. She wrapped the delicate, Grant-era pieces in tissue and packed them for Rachel. Someone with a different aesthetic would love them.

She stood in her small living room, deciding where to put a tree, when a loud engine, idling in the alley below, drowned out her music. A bright glare from below lit up her ceiling. A car door opened, and a low murmur of voices filled the alley before a door closing cut off the sound. Mari stepped out onto the balcony and leaned over the railing to see what was going on.

A huge black pickup truck shifted into reverse and began to back up the narrow alley toward the avenue. Below her stood Jack, lit up by the truck's headlights, Soldier at his feet, his left hand around the trunk of a perfect noble fir about six feet tall. In the glare, its branches sparkled with thousands of tiny raindrops.

"Are you nuts?" she called down to him.

He tipped his face up to her. No dark glasses. "You wanted a tree."

The backing truck reached the top of the alley, then its tail dipped down into the street, and the bright beam of its headlights swung up and away, leaving Jack in shadowy darkness. He stood straight, letting the rain soak him, offering his gift without words.

He was alone except for the dog. There was no Bradley or other security person.

"I'm coming down," she said.

She shoved her feet into flip-flops and hurried down the stairs.

In the alley, her gaze met his naked, open one, and she couldn't remember why she was so angry with him. She wanted a tree: Jack brought her a tree. Grandpa Connor needed help: Jack took her to him. Jack didn't explain. He acted. One minute he drove her crazy, the next he melted her heart.

"You're alone." She stopped a few feet from him. "No SUV, no team?"

"Supposed to focus. Can't," he said.

It was one of those times when his speech seemed to come from far away. She didn't know what he was supposed to focus on. "How did you get here?"

"Walked."

"With the tree?" Mari was confused. He and the dog were certainly wet.

"Mae brought it." As soon as he said it, she remembered the big black truck from Mae's driveway. He lifted the tree and held it out to her as if it weighed no more than one of Rachel's small bouquets. "For you."

"Come inside."

"If you want me…to."

"You're soaked."

He didn't move. She recognized the frozen stillness of his posture, the man who needed to keep his balance. Mari went to him and took the tree. Drops from the cold wet needles hit her PJs, making her shiver. She set the tree on its wooden stand where the path along the side of the house led to her door. Jack wasn't going to ask for help, but she thought he might accept it. She went to his side and slipped her arm in his and waited. There was a dry spot of warmth where her arm met his ribs through the shirt. Everywhere else was wet and cool.

"Ready?" she asked.

He gave Soldier a command, and the three of them moved down the path to her open door. He looked up the steep, narrow stairs to her living room, his mouth set in a grim, determined line.

She left him standing at her door while she retrieved the tree. "I'll go ahead. Does Soldier need anything?"

"No," he said.

She started up the stairs, lugging the tree, its tip pointing up, the branches wet and prickly against her body. Behind her, Jack gave the dog a command to stay. About halfway up, the wooden stand caught on a tread, and she stopped to adjust her hold. Abruptly, the heavy base came free of the step, lightening her burden. Over the branches, she could see the top of Jack's head and his grip on the stair rail.

She set the tree down across from her loveseat, next to the low half-wall that separated her eating area from the living room. The evergreen scent filled the apartment. Her T-shirt stuck to her in wet patches dotted with fir needles. She pulled the wet shirt away from her body, shaking off the needles, and turned to find Jack standing with his back braced against the room's inner wall, facing her, his eyes closed, face taut. Rain dripped from his hair to his shoulders, from his pant cuffs to her floor, and his eyes opened as if he'd felt her gaze.

"Take off your shirt," she told him. That was the sensible, practical thing to do.

He gave her his faint shadow smile.

"I'll toss it in the dryer." She went for a towel from her bathroom. When she returned, he still wore the shirt. His fingers fumbled with the small dark buttons slick with rain. She tossed the towel aside and closed her hands over his. "You're too cold. Let me."

He dropped his hands to his sides. Mari worked the buttons free of the stiff, wet wool, her fingers brushing against his chest. His head rested against the wall, and his eyes closed. She didn't think he breathed. A slight tremor stirred him. Under the wet wool of his outer shirt, a charcoal-gray tee clung to his skin. She pushed the edges of the outer shirt toward his shoulders. His eyes opened, and he came away from the wall, letting her strip off the shirt.

She stepped back, holding it against her chest, her gaze fixed on him. He pulled the gray T-shirt off and let it fall to the floor. His hair, wet and tangled, revealed the sinuous inky lines of the tattoos on his neck, like a flowing script. Her gaze dropped to his long, lean torso, his skin pebbled from the cold. Faint puckered scars marred his ribs. Mari had an appalled thought that they were burn scars from the tip of a lighted cigarette. The wet khakis sagged around his hips and clung to his legs and groin. A small black box hooked to his waistband, some sort of communication device, reminded her that he remained connected to his security team.

He touched the box. "Off. No cameras," he said. "No guards."

She raised her gaze to meet his. "You must think I'm easily won—one perfect Christmas tree—and I melt. My anger at your controlling ways just dissolves."

"I have no control. I can't stay away."

He reached for her and pulled her against him, awkwardly trapping her arms and the shirt between them. She pushed back, dropping the shirt and freeing her arms to slide around him, yielding to the pull of him, as she had wanted to do from the first, against sense and reason. He was lean and solid and smelled of rain and Christmas tree. Her breasts flattened against his chest. He grabbed the hem of her T-shirt, yanking it up so that skin met skin. She sucked in a breath and turned her face up to his.

He kissed her, his mouth warm, his skin icy cold. The kiss was hungry, reckless, and imprecise. He moved to make their mouths fit more completely, and she opened to him. He answered with a deeper kiss, stronger, more urgent.

She thought she knew sex, but this was different. The jolt of it hit her like a rough wave knocking her off her feet, lifting her, sucking her in, pulling her out beyond the point where her feet could touch bottom.

From the alley below came the sudden blare of a car alarm, and Mari broke their kiss with a jerk. Jack tensed instantly, pulling her back to him, pressing her cheek to his chest, his arms protecting her now. His chest rose and fell as if he'd been running hard. His heart raced in her ear as her breath gusted against his shoulder. He touched the box at his waist.

The alarm kept up its insistent blasts of sound. A second alarm started. By the time a third alarm went off, doors had opened, and Mari's neighbors shouted to one another in loud, annoyed voices.

"You and I get together and alarms go off. Literally." She tried to make a joke of it, to pull back in his arms. "I should go down. My car is one of them."

His hold tightened. "Don't. It's a ploy. My team will come. Secure the area."

The alley was full of voices now. Someone must have called the cops because the flash of red and blue lights from a police cruiser chased across her ceiling. She needed to get her keys from the kitchen counter, to go down to be among her neighbors. One of the alarms stopped. Jack still had a hand on the box at his waist.

"Can you tell me what the danger is?" She searched his face, but it was closed to her, showing nothing.

"You make me forget."

She touched the flowing line of a tattoo that slanted down the side of his throat and felt him swallow. "Are you under an evil curse like in a fairy tale?"

The last alarm fell silent. There was only the sound of a police radio and people talking.

Jack's hold slid away. "I made a promise."

Her heart sank. A promise was worse than a curse. A curse could be broken. He would do whatever the promise required of him, at whatever the cost.

"Decorate the tree," he said. He cupped her jaw in his hands.

She'd forgotten the tree. "Not without you."

Below them at the base of the stairs, Soldier gave a low whimper.

"They're here," Jack said. "I have to go."

He gave her one swift, hard kiss, put a hand to the wall, and pivoted away from her toward the stairs. Soldier came up to meet him. They descended, Jack with one hand on the rail and one on Soldier's harness, moving deliberately, one step at the time. From the bottom of the stairs, Jack looked up. "Don't go out. Wait for a text."

She nodded.

He stepped out into the night, and the door closed behind him. His discarded clothes lay in a wet heap on the floor at her feet, and she scooped them up and ran down the stairs. Her hand was on the door when a low, fierce voice on the other side stopped her.

"You're not supposed to be careless, Ryker," the deep male voice said. "You're supposed to make Evans careless."

There was no answer, only swift, quiet footsteps moving away from the alley toward the walk street. Above her on the kitchen counter, her phone pinged with a text. She climbed the stairs and checked the message. *All clear.*

The tree filled her apartment with its fragrance. Her gaze fell on the box of ornaments on the table, and she knew what was different about Jack. Grant hadn't broken her heart, could not have broken her heart. Jack could smash it to pieces.

Chapter 11

By Wednesday, nearly three days after Jack's unexpected, shirtless departure from her apartment, Mari was pretty sure she'd go nuts if she didn't stop thinking about him. Her reaction to him puzzled her. What she did know was puzzling and contradictory. Whatever had happened to him on the other side of the world had cast its shadow over the way he lived now, and he seemed to want to keep that part of his life in a separate compartment, a box, like the black box he wore on his hip.

They'd skipped all the dating preliminaries, all the "who do you know," "where did you go to school," "what are your favorites" kind of talk and gone straight to taking off each other's clothes. She wanted to go right back to where they'd left off—skin to skin, mouth to mouth.

At noon, she fled her office and dropped in on the annual Dickens show at the Book Nook's story hour. There a group of teenage actors bundled up in layers of Dickensian period costumes played to a full house of preschoolers and their moms, grandparents, and nannies. Outside the mall, it was a sunny southern California day, but inside, the actors shivered in a snowy London of long ago. The show, which ran with a different high school cast each week, was a Christmas tradition at the mall, one that Mari loved.

Seeing it was another reminder, like her box of old ornaments, of how wrong she and Grant had been as a couple. Grant liked to introduce her to his business school friends as the woman who kept the Coast Plaza Mall's numbers high. With his arm around her shoulders at parties, he'd prompt her to recite the mall's latest sales figures. His favorite number was revenue-per-square-foot-of-retail-space. "Awesome," he'd say and insist on a high five. She'd smile, but feel diminished. At the time she hadn't understood why. Her boyfriend was proud of her. He was showing her off to his friends. Until he wasn't, until when they were breaking up, and he told her she'd be left behind, clinging to her dead-end job. "Malls," he said. "So last century."

Now she looked at the rapt audience enjoying Dickens's story brought to life—that was her achievement, bringing people together. The mall was the place where she could do that. Grant had never understood what her job was about. He saw numbers and figures. She saw people and community. It was only natural. She came from a family that liked to gather. That's what made her attraction to an edgy recluse like Jack so strange.

"A merry Christmas, uncle," cried the boy playing Scrooge's nephew Fred in a top hat and long-tailed plaid coat.

"Bah," said the white-whiskered, bewigged teen playing Scrooge. "Humbug."

Fred winked at the girl with a ledger and quill pen, playing a hunched over Bob Cratchit. "Don't be cross, uncle."

The teen Scrooge went into his speech about Christmas being a time for paying bills without money and finding oneself a year older. "If I could work my will," he cried, pointing at his audience, "every idiot who goes about with 'Merry Christmas' on his lips should be boiled with his own pudding, and buried with a stake of holly through his heart."

The little ones, sitting on the floor or in the safety of cozy laps, gasped and giggled.

"But, uncle," answered Fred, "I've always thought of Christmas—as a good time; a kind, forgiving, charitable, pleasant time; a time when men and women open their hearts freely to their neighbors, and I say, 'God bless it.'"

The female Bob Cratchit applauded heartily, getting the audience to clap with her. Teen Scrooge glared fiercely at all of them and pronounced another "Bah. Humbug."

Mari was laughing when a worried-looking Shanny appeared at her side and silently held out her phone. A news feed ran with the sound off, and on the tiny screen, police officers in full protective gear herded people from a building. Maryrose whispered, "What is this?"

Shanny crooked a finger to have her follow, and they moved to the other side of the store.

"A computer store robbery in the middle of a mall. It's so frightening. The robbers just invaded," Shanny said, her face anxious.

"Where?"

"I don't know. It could be anywhere."

The screen flashed a location, and Mari handed Shanny's phone back. She put an arm around her friend's shoulders. "Okay. Breathe, Shanny. That's—what?—twenty miles away."

"But what if it's a trend? What if crooks are targeting malls, and we're next? We've got the same store."

"The good news is that if they're targeting high-end computer stores, they're not targeting bookstores." Mari glanced at the rapt group of little ones, lost in the old story. For them, the dangerous world of the twenty-first century had momentarily faded away. They were in Scrooge's cold counting house, watching the old man praise the jails, the workhouses, and the treadmill.

Mari pulled out her phone and checked with security. No alerts. At the mall, they'd adopted protocols recommended by the local police department, and they'd practiced for all types of emergencies. She had no doubt that the head of mall security already knew about the distant situation. Meanwhile, she needed to calm her friend.

"Listen, Shanny. We're going to be okay. Close your news feed. The police are there handling that situation. Concentrate on the kids right here, and I'll get security to send someone over to the store so you're not alone." She gave Shanny another quick hug.

Shanny clicked out of the news feed and offered Mari a wobbly smile. "Okay, thanks, Mari. The world just seems so dangerous, and I want everyone to be happy at Christmas."

"Me too, Shanny." Mari nodded. "So, let's do what we do to spread the joy. Look at those kids. You're doing it."

Shanny returned to the sales counter, and Mari texted the head of mall security. He replied that they would send an armed security person to the bookstore. When she looked up from her phone, Shanny was chatting with a gray-haired woman wearing a deep green sweater and a reindeer antlers headband. Mari turned to leave, then stopped.

Out of nowhere except maybe her own head, Jack appeared. He stood between the twin white columns of the merchandise surveillance system at the store entrance, Soldier at his side. Mari thought all the alarms ought to beep.

"What are you doing here?" Mari asked. Out of the corner of her eye she saw Shanny glance their way.

"Shopping." He wore the dark glasses, and his mouth had the tight look she now recognized as the strain of trying to keep his balance. A particularly jazzy version of "Jingle Bells" came from the mall sound system. Across the passageway, Bradley's cinder block profile filled a window. She understood. Something in Jack's past had made him, like Shanny, a kind of human seismometer, hypersensitive to the world's dangers.

"You heard there was a robbery," she said. "At a mall twenty miles away?"

His mouth quirked upward briefly. His physical presence, an arm's length away, had its usual effect on her, waking her senses. From behind his dark glasses, she felt the directness of his gaze. A memory surfaced of being in charge of the old radio on her grandpa's boat and fiddling with the dial until she hit on the right frequency. Whatever her head thought, her body said that Jack was her personal right frequency.

Shanny stepped up and linked her arm through Mari's. She gave Jack a cool, full-body assessment. "May I help you?" she asked.

"Shannon, this is Jack." Mari extracted her arm from her friend's protective hold. "Jack, Shannon is the Coast Plaza Book Nook manager."

"Oh." Shanny's eyebrows went up. "Hi," she said stiffly. She leaned toward him and spoke quietly. "You're in security, right? So, you heard about the robbery? What do you think? Are we safe here?"

"Shanny," Mari protested, tugging her friend back. "Mall security is not Jack's job."

"My team is looking into it." His mouth was grim.

Behind them, the teen version of Marley's ghost rattled his chains, and little voices squealed in delicious mock fright, which was, after all, the best kind of fright.

"Excuse us, Shanny." Mari gave her friend a pointed look.

"Okay." Shanny backed off. "Just saying, it'd be great to have more security. Nice to meet you, Jack."

Over Jack's shoulder, Mari could see Officer Wiggs approaching, looking crisp and professional in his blue uniform shirt and tie, a weapon on his hip. He strolled up the wide center aisle of the mall, greeting people, and stopped just before he reached the bookstore to take a last swig of his coffee drink and toss the cup into a trash receptacle.

"Hey, Ms. Lynch," he said. "Got a problem?" He gave Jack a hard stare.

"Not at all, Officer." Mari smiled. "Shannon wants you nearby. That's all, thanks."

"Sure, miss."

Wiggs sauntered over to the sales counter, and Mari turned to Jack. She had to admit that Jack deserved a suspicious scrutiny. He looked dangerous. It wasn't the black, ribbed-knit sweater or the dark glasses, or even the chin-length hair that didn't quite cover the tattoos on his neck. There was a quality of menace in his immovable stance. She wanted him away from Wiggs. "Shall we walk?" she invited.

He and Soldier pivoted. Mari was growing accustomed to the way he moved. She linked her arm in his. They strolled down the mall away from the bookstore. Whatever Jack had been doing, he'd left it and come to check on her. That was one thing she did know about him—he had a wide protective streak.

"We do have security at the mall," Mari told him.

"I saw," he said. "My guys are better."

She glanced over at Bradley as they passed him. He shot her a distinctly hostile glance. It occurred to her that Jack's team might not be happy about Jack's secret visit to her apartment. They'd certainly hurried him away, and he'd kept away too, until now. "Your guys are not on our payroll."

"Nevertheless…" Jack said.

She laughed. "I thought I was the only one who used that word. What's so wrong with our security?"

He didn't hesitate. "Too many ways in and out. Guards who don't see danger, aren't even looking for it. Security cameras easily evaded. Everyone sticking to the same routines."

"Oh." The rapid flow of words, so unlike his usual clipped, intermittent speech, surprised her. She'd been trying to figure out his way of speaking since they'd first met. She still didn't know how to explain it, whether the difficulty was the words getting in or getting out.

Halfway down the south wing of the mall, they stopped outside of a popular, high-end cookware store. Inside, customers, arms sagging under heavy shopping bags, milled around the displays. A tantalizing sugary smell came from some baking demo.

"I want to see you again," Jack said.

"You do see me. I'm right here." She knew that wasn't what he meant. His nearness and the sexy subtext of the words had her body humming with awareness in spite of their very public setting.

The smell of gingerbread and hot apple cider wafted over them from the cookware shop. Mari glanced around. No danger seemed imminent in the crowd of mostly women shoppers. Bradley and two other black-shirted hulks, who looked suspiciously like members of Jack's security team, had stationed themselves nearby. "Maybe, if you're so worried about security, we should meet somewhere very safe…where we can talk and—"

"Talk?" The word came out on a rasp.

"…get to know one another better. There's little sitting park behind the police station." It was a postage-stamp-size park surrounded by the police station, the library, and city hall, very private.

"The police station?"

"I was teasing."

"I'm serious," he said. "This is a bad place for us to…talk."

"Oh, too much distraction." For a moment she had forgotten how difficult the mall was for him. His arm, warm and solid against her side, seemed perfectly steady. The black sweater hugged his shoulders and torso and bulged over the box attached to his waistband.

He didn't answer at once. "You distract me." He dropped his arm. Their hands met, and he entwined her fingers with his in a warm clasp.

She swallowed. She wanted to press her whole body against his. "We should talk, you know, not…just fall into each other's arms. You could tell me about your video game."

After a pause, he answered, "I could. And you?"

"You know too much about me already."

"Tell me something I don't know, then." His voice dropped to a low register.

Mari closed her eyes. She opened them to stare through the store window at a display of knife sets. Hundreds of dollars' worth of very sharp steel. She shook off the sexual daze, disengaged her hold, and turned to face him squarely. "Want to hear about my skill with a filleting knife? You have no idea what I can do with a sharp knife and a twelve-pound salmon."

"Something your grandpa taught you?"

"I'll tell you about it tonight." She leaned in close to his ear. "City hall sitting park. Eight?"

"Eight."

***

Jack stood next to the black SUV in the silence of the parking lot, waiting for Mari to finish work. He breathed the cool evening air. His senses needed time to recover from a long afternoon of the mall's assault on them. He'd backed off from seeing her for almost three days, but now he wouldn't wait any longer.

After the episode at her apartment, Rashaad had been direct with him. *You've got to come clean with that girl, man. You're getting in deep without her knowing who you really are. You want her to be safe? Tell her who you are, and let her choose if she wants to be with you.*

Rashaad was right, but Jack wanted another date with her before he risked her turning away and going back to her world. Today when robbers had boldly invaded a mall computer store, Jack had been unable to stay away. Violence had tentacles that could reach into the most ordinary life. Borders and guards and TSA lines at the airport didn't keep out the world's dangers. So he'd struck a bargain with his team to have this night with her in exchange for telling her the truth about who he was.

The box at his waist buzzed. Bradley had spotted Mari leaving her office. Jack positioned himself beyond the pool of light illuminating the exit. She didn't think as he did. She had no Frank Evans in her life. She hadn't learned to vary the pattern of her movements to avoid being followed. She'd close up her office and walk out the nearest mall exit without a thought for any danger.

The guys had nixed the idea of the little sitting park by the police station as a meeting place, but Jack had a plan. He'd thought of a safe place, a place Evans knew nothing about. The place had been in the back of Jack's mind from the moment he'd smelled his first Christmas tree in eleven years. Standing in the rain, wrapped in the fresh green smell, had loosened a flood of memories. And then her question about the video game made everything come together. During the long afternoon, he'd made a couple of purchases and phone calls to arrange things. All he needed when she appeared was to persuade her to trust him enough to go along with the new plan.

From one of the building's rear entrances, she emerged with her car key in hand. A silver snowflake pin on the lapel of her tailored red wool jacket flashed in the light, and her silky flowered skirts swirled around her legs. He had a moment to watch her unobserved, liking her glad, purposeful stride as she headed for him. His heartbeat, which he had disciplined to strict regularity, gave a funny skip.

When she saw him, she halted a few feet away, not startled, but wary. She leveled a steady, accusing gaze at him. "You never left the mall, did you?"

How could he on the day of a robbery even if the robbers hadn't harmed anyone and they'd operated miles away? He was supposed to explain. The guys expected him to explain, but he wanted to hold her, not scare her away. He held up the bag with his purchase. "Something for you."

She glanced at the store logo on the bag, looking puzzled. "For me?"

"You wanted me to tell you about the game. I could teach you."

"Oh. I'd like that." She smiled. The warmth of it momentarily distracted him.

"Will you come, then?" He stretched out a hand.

Her gaze shifted to the SUV behind him. "Where to this time?" she asked.

He looked away. "A quiet place. Not dangerous."

"No sofas, then?"

His gaze shot back to her. She saw through him. There was a sofa, all right, and he planned to spend a lot of time on it with her. "One or two."

"Your team will be there?"

"Nearby."

"Just so we're clear," she said, accepting his hand at last. "We won't be having sex on a couch with them hovering nearby, pretending not to notice."

"I think I can manage that." In truth, he wasn't ready for sex. He hadn't figured out how to ditch the team in order to duck into the nearest pharmacy for condoms. They were on to him after his brief solo venture to bring her a tree. Still, his plan to teach her to play the video game meant he would get close to her, very close.

Chapter 12

Once again, Mari sat seat-belted in the back of the SUV, beside Jack and Soldier. When she'd surrendered her purse and phone to Bradley, she couldn't escape the feeling that she'd interrupted another argument between Jack and his team. This time Bradley also took her car key, explaining that she'd find the car in her parking spot when she got home.

She wanted to fume that all this security was unnecessary. She couldn't imagine that her little beach town harbored any real threat to Jack or anyone else, but she remained silent. There was something going on between Jack and his security team that she didn't understand. They drove inland, zigzagging from residential neighborhoods lined with parked cars and decorated with lights to the high occupancy vehicle lane of the 405 freeway and back. As before, the driver had a light touch on the brakes. Mari gave up trying to orient herself, and realized that was the point. It was evasive driving, as if the driver anticipated someone following them.

She held the bag with Jack's purchase on her lap, arguing with herself about the unwisdom of setting off with him again against the happy feeling of being near him. The ride was a brief blur, but she was sure they were far from the beach when the car slowed and turned down a long, narrow alley and into a short driveway. A garage door opened, and they entered an enormous, well-lit garage that echoed the style of the old California missions with cream-colored walls and dark wood beams. Four cars with college decals and racks for bikes and surfboards occupied one half of the space as if a normal active family lived there, and yet there was plenty of room for the SUV. Mari couldn't help thinking that her dad would have serious garage envy.

The SUV's doors popped open, and Bradley hopped out of the front seat and vanished through an interior door. At Jack's command, Soldier leapt down, and Jack reached up for a smooth black metal bar she hadn't noticed before and pulled himself up out of his seat with a quick flex of his arms. He pivoted with his whole body, a move she now recognized, and used another bar on the top of the doorframe to swing down out of the car, almost like a gymnast. What he never did, she realized, was to make rapid head movements. He turned to her from the center of the garage, his face expressionless, a sign he'd gone into his radio-silence mode again.

She followed him out of the car, taking the bag with her. "Where are we?"

He didn't answer, appearing to listen for something beyond the door through which Bradley had vanished. The SUV's doors shut, making Mari start. The driver came around the front, and she recognized him as the hunky, dark-haired, dark-skinned waiter of their dinner date. He strode past them. "Perimeter check in progress," he said and followed where Bradley had gone.

To Mari, it seemed as if she and Jack were actors on a screen, and someone had hit "pause" on a remote to freeze them in place. It couldn't have been more than two minutes, however, before footsteps and voices approached from the other side of the door. One was Bradley's, the other was female and excited.

Jack tensed. "Wait here," he said to Maryrose. He ordered Soldier to protect her and stepped through the door. The excited female voice cried out, "*Hijo*." Something crashed and shattered, and the door shut, closing off a burst of Spanish and English that sounded half scolding and half endearment.

Mari and Soldier were alone in the garage, so she reached down to let him sniff her hand. "Well, Soldier," she said. "He may not be easy to know, but someone likes your master." The dog gave her hand a lick.

When the door opened again, Jack beckoned her in. "Come."

Mari didn't move. "Is everyone okay?"

"Yes." He flashed her one of his fleeting smiles.

She moved toward him but stopped short of taking the hand he offered. "You really should tell me where we are."

He gave the floor mat at her feet a thorough scrutiny. It was one of those moments she could never quite predict when his unwillingness to admit something about his past broke their connection. At last he spoke. "My parents' house."

At the words, she remembered his dead parents, his mother who'd been fond of room service, and his father who was simply *gone.* He'd brought her to a place that was another marker of absence and loss in his life, and she, without meaning to, had touched an unhealed wound.

She put her hand in his then and let him tug her in his wake as they passed through a hall and out again onto a large patio with a pool. The shopping bag banged against her knee, and Soldier trotted behind. Outdoor lights illuminated an imposing two-story house in the old Spanish Colonial style. They passed through a French door into a large kitchen with miles of tiled countertops, lit only by the glow of dials on appliances, and smelling of something sweet and buttery, and then on into the dark house. Jack moved with the easy familiarity of someone who knew the way.

He opened the door to a high-ceilinged room, easily twice the size of Mari's apartment. The soft glow of wall sconces illuminated dark wood-paneled walls, bookcases, and a vast parquet floor. Along one wall stood a bar where a tray of cookies and drinks had been placed. From the warm, sugary scent of them, the cookies must have just come from the kitchen. A pool table dominated the far side of the room, and in front of Mari a long tufted white velvet sofa faced a wall-mounted TV screen as large as her mother's dining table.

"Do you need anything?" he asked.

A minute to rearrange my thoughts about who you are. She wondered how many rooms there were and how many acres surrounded the place. "You grew up here?"

"Do you like it?"

It wasn't the question she was expecting. As usual, it wasn't his words but his actions that revealed him. He'd just exposed her in the most direct possible way to the gulf between them, really a major chasm. He'd seen her apartment. He'd seen her grandfather's modest bungalow. He knew her net worth. He probably knew the balance on her college loans.

"There were other houses?" she guessed, houses full of staff.

"Palm Springs. Montecito. Puerto Vallarta."

She turned to him, and a surge of sympathy made her heart ache, which was dumb. Apparently, he'd never been ordinary. He'd seemed within reach in her apartment, wet from the rain in his surfer's board shirt and flip-flops, but that was an illusion. He'd grown up in a palace. More than one, apparently, in places associated with the glamour of old Hollywood. Now he lived in a virtual prison. She didn't want to, but she might have to accept what the clues were telling her about her mystery man—they had nothing in common except a very hot attraction to one another.

"Who called you *hijo* just now?" She knew the Spanish word for *son*.

"Paloma Gomez, my nanny from when I was four until… Now she and her family live here. In the guest house. She and her husband manage…the property."

"She knew you were coming. She made everything ready, but when she saw you, she dropped something. What?"

"A plate of cookies." He didn't look at her.

Mari set the shopping bag at her feet and closed the distance between them. She laid her hands on his chest, waiting for his gaze to come back to her. Under her touch, his chest was taut with whatever feelings he suppressed. "Paloma was shocked at your appearance? Because…" More bits and pieces of things he'd said about his past swirled in Mari's head. The real mystery was what had happened to him between the palace of his lost family and the locked fortress he now lived in. "How long has it been since Paloma last saw you?"

"Eleven years."

Mari swallowed. She could neither move nor speak. *Eleven years*. He had been a boy when he left home. Paloma, who had loved him then, must love him still. She had dropped a plate, shocked to see the woundedness of the man. Mari leaned her head against his chest and spoke as lightly as she could. "Well, then, that explains it. You show up at Paloma's door with tattoos on your neck, badly in need of a haircut. Any self-respecting nanny would be appalled."

A single spasm of laughter shook him. His arms came around her, and he kissed the top of her head. "You changed your shampoo," he said.

"It's peppermint," she said. "For Christmas time."

"I like it."

For a while they simply stood there. She held herself perfectly still, asking nothing, but hoping he would tell her anyway. When he didn't speak, she slipped out of his hold and perched on the edge of the couch.

"What's in the bag?" she asked, as if it didn't matter that he wouldn't tell her about his past. She pulled out a plastic-wrapped disk, which he took from her. He waved her to the white sofa while he opened a cabinet under the huge TV and slipped the disk into some sort of player. The screen came to life.

Jack pulled a small, two-legged, black plastic device from a drawer in the cabinet and handed it to Mari. "It's a game controller," he said, "an older model, but it still works. I asked Paloma's son Javier to set it up for you this afternoon. He plays in English, and like you, he doesn't have any physical impairments."

"I haven't done this, you know, played these games." She recognized the controller from a display in the mall's high-tech gadget store. She held it in her lap, trying to make sense of its controls.

"I'll teach you." He sat down next to her on the couch, his shoulder against hers, and guided her hands into position on the small controller. "Thumbs on the joysticks," he said. "Index fingers on the triggers."

He was close, and he smelled wonderful: male and citrusy. His touch on her hands sent currents of sensation zinging through her. "Triggers?" she asked. "Is it a shooting game?"

"Technically. It's called *Rescue Force.* You could call it a 'first-person shooter' game, but mainly in this game, the players use the triggers for actions other than shooting."

"And the joysticks?" She experimented, nudging the small, flexible raised buttons with her thumbs.

"The left one lets you move in the world of the game; the right one lets you look in different directions."

"And these?" Mari ran her right thumb across a set of four bright-colored buttons, labeled A B X Y.

"They are preprogrammed with moves you can make, like picking something up or opening a door." He was talking about something other than himself, and she noticed how easily the words came.

"Show me," she said.

"Turn on the power." He indicated a button. She pushed it, and a new screen appeared on the TV. He indicated another button, which she pushed, and the screen changed until a few lines of text popped up, explaining that *Rescue Force* had been developed with the help of a research team at a London university to improve a player's cognitive flexibility. A smaller font indicated that profits from game sales went to a foundation to support brain-injured veterans.

She turned to look at him. His profile was as uncommunicative as usual. Josh Huntington had called Jack a philanthropist, but Mari could see that he wasn't owning the label.

"Keep pushing," he advised.

He reached across her to tap a button. She pulled her hand away to give him access, and his arm collided briefly with her breast. At the fleeting touch, she sucked in a quick sharp breath. He withdrew his hand, and she let the pent breath go, trying to concentrate on the screen.

The screen changed again to a setting like a hospital corridor with a mint-green linoleum floor, a gurney against one tan wall, and wide double doors under a glowing red Exit sign. A bit of text said that on any given day, somewhere in the world, militants held AMCITS, American citizens, hostage. The next line invited player Mari to join *Rescue Force* and save the hostages. A soundtrack of wailing heavy metal music swelled.

"You can play this game?" She wondered about his sensitivity to noise and light.

"There are some extra controls that I use." He tapped a button and the movement on the screen froze. "That's one I use. There are others if a player needs them, and a player can create a character a lot like himself or herself, and the game takes those limits and abilities into account."

A small four-pointed starburst below the Exit sign beckoned. Mari pushed the left joystick, expecting to move forward, but nothing happened. Jack tapped a colored button, and a new screen appeared. "First, you have to create your character."

She fumbled with the buttons through a series of onscreen menus that invited her to choose her character's gender, appearance, abilities, and vulnerabilities. He leaned back against the sofa, watching her. After a few attempts, she got the hang of the controls to make selections. When she'd created a short, buff female named Ginger, an inactive marine, with a prosthetic right arm and a sensitivity to sudden loud noises, she turned to him.

A tiny smile appeared at the corner of his mouth. "You're doing great. Ready for some hostages?"

She nodded. He leaned forward and tapped a button. The background music faded, and a scene appeared of three ragged, bearded men huddled together against a rough dirty wall. Faint light from a small high window illuminated their bowed heads. They shivered as a wind howled. It was a game, but it looked very real. A text line identified them as two American contractors and their translator, missing fathers and sons. The men didn't appear to be shackled. As she looked closer, what had seemed to be a crack in the wall above them turned out to be a line of black flowing script. A chill of recognition passed through her. She'd seen that kind of script before, disguised and hidden by a man's longish hair, but the same. The scene was not entirely the product of someone's imagination. It was partly a specific man's memory.

"What does it say on the wall?" she asked.

Jack's thumb brushed the back of her hand, and the screen disappeared. "Maybe a different set of hostages." He worked the buttons until the screen showed an older-style passenger jet on a dirt tarmac with a background of dense green jungle behind it.

"Wait." She pushed his hand aside, holding him by the wrist. "Tell me about the wall."

An interminable pause followed. Mari's heart thudded in her chest at her own boldness. At last, he let his hand drop.

"It says—*cowards and infidel dogs die*." His voice was neutral, empty of emotion. He offered no explanation, no new information.

She wanted to know so many things—*is that what you were, a contractor? How long were you kept in that hut? How did you get out?* But what she said was, "Right. Thank you. We have to save them."

After another silence, he guided her hand to one of the colored buttons. "Let's pick your squad."

He led her into the world of the game. As Ginger, she made a squad out of a retired marine sergeant with sniper capabilities, a shaggy gray, three-legged, bomb-sniffing dog, and a teenage villager with cousins in New York. Jack didn't question her choices. While the dog and the teen gathered intelligence on the hostages' situation, Ginger had a choice to go it alone or to involve her squad members. Every time she chose to rely on her team, Jack pointed out how she gained mysterious points in a display on the screen.

"You are more powerful with a team," he told her. "Now you plan."

There were menus with an array of feints or ruses Ginger's team could use. Again, Mari discovered that the game rewarded Ginger's second choices or her team's suggestions. *Flexibility,* that was the key.

"Ready for the assault?" he asked. "It gets crazy now."

"What if I mess up?"

"You die," he said.

"Thanks, that's helpful."

"And it's a game, so you get to start over," he said. "Come here." He took hold of her waist and lifted her across his thigh to nestle in the vee between his splayed legs. He pulled her back against his groin. His arms came around her. He fit his hands over hers on the game controls. His heart beat against her left shoulder blade. His arousal was a distinct ridge against her hip.

"So," she said, "this game is an excuse to seduce me."

He froze. "If it were just us, no guards, no dog, would you mind?"

"Mind?" She wondered how he could not tell how turned on she was, had been from the moment he'd brushed against her breast. Maybe even from the moment she'd climbed into the car next to him.

She set aside the controller and twisted around to face him, kneeling, bracing her hands on the back of the sofa. He was sitting with his usual erect posture, the tattoos on his neck plainly visible, his eyes wide and looking deeply into hers.

"Just so you know," she said. She leaned forward and kissed him, gently at first, in the hollow of his neck where the black lines snaked across his skin. She meant only to show him that she, too, felt the pull of their connection, but he asked for more. He gripped her waist and drew her to him, lifting his face until their mouths met in a hungry, searching kiss that lasted somewhere between forever and mere heartbeat. With a groan Jack broke the kiss, running his hands up over her ribs to her breasts. Under the brush of his thumbs, her nipples grew taut, and she arched to give him access until he took one silk-clad breast in his heated mouth. Wild bolts of sensation streaking through her made her knees buckle. She sank down and gave her mouth up to his again. Another lost interlude followed until

Soldier shook, and the little jingle of his collar brought Mari back to reality.

"Stop." She pulled back to look at him. Their ragged breath mingled, and he looked as mindless as she felt. "We're not doing this now. We have hostages to save."

She brushed his lips once with a gentle kiss and settled back in his hold, pulling a throw pillow onto her lap and resting the controller on it, trembling with frustrated desire. She waited for him to come back to reality too. After a minute, his hold came around her again, his hands covering hers on the controls.

For the next stretch of time, they made Ginger run and dodge, crouch and leap, throw smoke devices, and lead her team. At every turn, unexpected snags forced Ginger to make new choices. Whenever Ginger made an adjustment, her team advanced.

As Ginger's team closed in on the hut where the hostages were kept, the dog drove a small herd of goats to forage in some nearby dead grass. Two armed men emerged to wave the goats away. A hidden IED up the road went off, exploding a concealed cache of arms. The two militants trotted up the road, shouting and brandishing their automatic weapons.

Mari had only a second to think how real the action was. The game required all her concentration, even as it occurred to her that by playing it, she was rewriting Jack's history.

A second explosion came from the back of the hut accompanied by the sound of falling bricks and a billowing black cloud of acrid smoke. The three hostages stumbled from the hut, doubled over, coughing, but alive. The dog guided them away. Ginger tossed a smoke bomb to cover their retreat over a stone wall. From the other end of the village, a short convoy of tan armored MTRVs approached, each with a marine gunner in position on the roof. A helicopter appeared overhead. The game's wailing guitar music theme swelled.

Mari collapsed back against Jack's chest, breathless, unprepared for the exhilaration of winning.

"You liked it," he said. His solid body made a safe circle around her. Sometime during the game, Soldier had settled at their feet, his chin on Mari's toes; then he lifted his head, alert, and in the next second, a knock came on the door. Bradley entered. "Time to get Ms. Lynch home safe," he said.

Somehow Mari got up off the couch. This time Bradley led the way back through the darkened house and into the kitchen. A substantial cardboard box that hadn't been there before sat on the kitchen island. A yellow sticky note on the box simply read "JACK." He stopped behind Mari as Bradley scooped up the box under one massive arm and kept moving.

"Wait," Jack said, then he vanished back into the interior of the house. Bradley communicated with someone on his wire. Then Jack reappeared with the cookies. "We can't leave them," he said. He handed Mari a large soft chocolate chip cookie.

When they reached the garage, there were two SUVs. Mari glanced from one to the other as Bradley led her to the nearest one. As she climbed in, she caught a bit of urgent conversation between Jack and another one of Jack's team who herded Jack toward the second SUV.

"You didn't tell her?"

Mari didn't hear Jack's answer, only the brief, crude outburst that followed. "That's it, man. You knew the deal: she doesn't know, you don't see her."

The door closed, the SUV pulled out of the garage, and they were off.

"Hello." Mari reached forward and tapped Bradley on the shoulder. "What just happened?"

"We always take two cars, miss," he said. "Best to buckle up."

Mari did as he suggested. The problem with loving Jack Ryker, she reflected, was that one could be left alone in the dark with a cookie.

Chapter 13

Late Friday morning, Jack took a call from Huntington. As Huntington described the quick favor he wanted, Jack eyed the cardboard box from Paloma. He had been treating the box like a bit of unexploded ordnance in a farmer's field, but the box could wait. The mission to find and arrest Evans had come to a temporary halt due to a major case that tied up all agents from the LA field office, including Agent Arias. The latest files Jack's team had sent Arias on Evans remained untouched, and now the message was, "I'll get back to you."

Half an hour later after the usual evasive driving by Miguel, Jack sat on the newspaper-covered floor of a garage up on the Palos Verdes hill while six ten-week-old yellow lab puppies climbed around and over him and Soldier. The favor Huntington wanted was help picking a puppy as a Christmas present for Max, his young, soon-to-be stepson. The puppies nuzzled, licked, and crawled on Jack, while Huntington talked in his easy way with the woman who'd bred them.

Nancy, a fit-looking, jeans-wearing redhead in her late fifties, handed Huntington a clipboard and a questionnaire for prospective buyers. She announced that she didn't sell puppies to just anyone and shrewdly questioned Huntington about his potential as a dog companion. When Huntington admitted he'd never had a dog, Nancy snatched back her clipboard and started to scold. Jack sent Soldier to sit obediently at Huntington's feet. Under the dog's steady influence, Nancy calmed down and returned the clipboard to Huntington, who rattled on with his usual breezy confidence. He had a way of getting what he wanted without appearing to push or demand. By the time he finished explaining about Emma and her kid Max and the promise that the boy could have a dog, Nancy was ready to give away the whole litter.

One pup kept coming back for more of Jack's attention, smelling his feet and tugging on Jack's shirt sleeve with tiny teeth. Jack cradled the friendly pup and dropped a set of keys to see how the dog reacted. Then he rolled a lime green tennis ball across the garage floor. The pup chased it down until it disappeared under a workbench. He dropped to his belly, on the floor, his nose under the bench, his rear in the air, one paw under the workbench. When he couldn't retrieve the ball, he barked at the offending bench, and Jack sent Soldier to help. The older dog went around the side of the workbench, dropped down, and reached under with a longer paw, flicking the ball out into the open. The puppy snatched it up, his tiny mouth barely able to hold it, and paraded with his little tail straight up in the air. Jack rewarded Soldier with a treat from his pocket, and the puppy dropped the ball and went straight for Jack, tugging at his khakis and squirming up into Jack's lap. Jack laughed. "This one."

Huntington asked to borrow Nancy's phone. "Okay, hold him, Ryker. Let me get a picture for Emma."

While Huntington and Nancy collected the wandering puppies and exchanged information about the dog's needs and the timing of the pickup, Jack got himself up off the floor. With the puppies back in their enclosure, Nancy saw the men out the door.

On the way down the hill toward the beach, Huntington talked on, apparently randomly, about Mae Sloan keeping the puppy so that he and Emma could surprise Max on Christmas Eve. Jack half-listened, thinking about Mari and how badly he kept screwing up with her.

"Hey, you should come to Mae's on Christmas Eve," Huntington said. "Bring Mari. Mae's quite impressed with her."

At the mention of Mari's name, Jack's groin tightened, an instant reminder of how deprived his body felt after two days without seeing her.

"How's that whole thing going, by the way?" Huntington asked.

"I screwed things up. But you suspected that, didn't you?" Huntington couldn't know the worst of it, but he had spoken with Mae and probably heard the story of Mari's missing grandpa. The Christmas Eve invitation, so casually thrown out, was not casual at all. Huntington had set him up, and just like Nancy, the puppy lady, Jack had been snowed by the old Huntington charm.

"Had to check on you. You're a pretty predictable guy, Ryker."

Jack had a passing thought that being predictable wasn't good for a man facing Frank Evans, but Huntington already had another potshot ready.

"I know what Headmaster Chambers did to Sloan. What did he do to you, Ryker?"

"Chambers?" At the mention of their former headmaster, Jack tensed, which was never good for his balance. "You think I'm screwed up because of Chambers?"

"It starts there. At seventeen, you were so angry you burned down the school sign. You were so angry you refused to go to…where was it? Some school back east."

"I think you picked a good pup," Jack said, making a bid to change the conversation.

"Nice try, Ryker," Huntington said. "You want to know what I think?"

"You're going to tell me."

"Chambers hurt your mother. That would be like him: to take advantage because she wanted to protect you."

Jack rarely turned his head, any sudden motion could set off an episode of dizziness that could take hours to overcome, but he had to look at Huntington. The guy was too perceptive.

"Her car was parked outside his office the night I burned the sign down," he admitted. He had been so rage-filled to see his mother alone with Chambers that he'd skipped graduation, and refused the spot he'd been offered at an East Coast Ivy.

Huntington nodded, but he didn't offer any phony sympathy.

In the year since Jack had returned to LA, Sloan had convinced Jack to give up his first scheme to destroy Chambers, which would have bankrupted the school. Instead, he and Sloan and Huntington had uncovered Chambers's long string of abuses against scholarship students, employees, and the school itself. A lot of the harm Chambers had done had been corrected or would be. The school was solvent again. Financial aid students, like Ulysses, the boy Sloan's wife Annie had helped, could attend Canyon without fear of harassment.

But some of Chambers's wrongs could never be undone. That was the thing that still enraged Jack, the reason he couldn't open the box Paloma had left for him. He realized now that his mother had not betrayed him. There had been no affair between her and the headmaster. She'd been in Chambers's office because she'd loved Jack. He had been powerless to protect her from the men in her life, from his father's infidelities, his coldness and disdain, and from Chambers's willingness to take advantage. It was Chambers who recommended the doctor who supplied his mother with meds until she took the dose that ended her life. At least Jack had fixed things so Chambers couldn't hurt any more kids or mothers.

Miguel pulled the SUV into the empty parking lot of a donut shop a block up from the Strand near Huntington's apartment at the low-rent end of the beach towns. For a few minutes, Jack and Huntington watched an aging, long-haired skateboarder practice jumps on and off an asphalt berm at the far end of the lot with a relentless repetition of the same moves. Seagulls checked out discarded bits of paper. The futility of simply repeating the same strategy struck Jack. Maybe he did need to open that box and be done forever with being messed up by Chambers. Jack gave the okay, and Bradley hopped out, opened Huntington's door, and handed Huntington back his phone.

Huntington opened the phone at once, checking his messages. "You want Mari to like you. So, you've got to be willing to let her see who you are—tattoos, scars, secrets, mistakes—all of it."

"Is that how you won Emma?"

"Yes." Huntington looked up from his phone, serious now. "The woman is totally immune to charm."

Jack pushed aside the hair over his collar, revealing the lines of ink on his neck. "You think I can tell her why I have these?"

"Listen, I don't know how bad you think you screwed up in that arms consulting business, but it's time to let it go."

"Good men died." That was the ugly fact. The thing Jack's arrogance had produced. He'd become cocky. He'd been sure he could operate in the murky world of arms dealing on the side of the good guys. He'd been wrong. The work Jack had done in other parts of the world bred ugly violence everywhere. He'd fallen for a front man and made the deal that had given Evans an opening. And when he'd pursued Evans for using that opening against US soldiers, Evans had followed Jack back to the ordinary world his friends inhabited. If he could find the words to tell Mari, she'd be repulsed.

Huntington shook his head, the simple gesture that Jack could no longer make. "Either you tell her, or you walk away. And I say let the past do its worst and be done with it. Oh, and come to Mae's Christmas Eve."

Jack didn't answer. The past waited for him. He meant to keep the promise he'd made. He would go after Evans until, like Chambers, Evans couldn't do any more harm.

Huntington held up his phone so Jack could see the picture on the screen. It was Jack holding the puppy, laughing. "By the way, I can always send her this pic, if you want her to see that inside that dark bitter shell of yours, there's a guy a dog can like."

***

Mari stared at her menu. Nothing appealed. Shanny and Rachel had insisted they meet for a late morning breakfast on Friday before another crazy pre-Christmas weekend in retail took over their lives. They sat in their favorite booth in a sunny corner of an upscale bistro adjacent to the mall. The place was famous for its muffins. Their server brought espresso drinks. The insubstantial little heart in the *crema* on top of Mari's coffee dissolved as she took her first sip.

"You've lost your Christmas spirit," Rachel said. "I don't even do Christmas, and I can tell."

Mari waited for menu inspiration. She should branch out, pick something new, a different omelet, or the avocado toast, but the new items came with mango salsa and six other garnishes, which she knew she would scrape off her food. "It's just a busy time, you know. Tomorrow's going to be crazy, and I'm not sure the Santa I've got lined up can handle a Saturday."

Their server returned, and Rachel and Shanny ordered. Mari was still looking at her menu when Rachel lifted it from her hands. "She'll have the spinach omelet with a side of fruit."

Mari. "I'm that predictable, am I?"

"It's your default dish. Talk to us, girl," said Rachel. "That's what we're here for."

"It's Jack, isn't it?" said Shanny. "He may be hot, but that doesn't make him right for you."

Mari stirred the last wisp of the heart-shaped cream in her cup. She'd been thinking in circles for three days. "I can't figure him out. But why am I trying, right? If I have to work so hard to read his signals, I'm kidding myself. He's not ready for a relationship, or he's just not that into me." That was the smart conclusion to make. Jack might not be willing to tell her about his past, but even without the telling, Mari knew the past had a tight hold on him. If he kept breaking their connection, something wasn't right.

Their server put a basket of hot oversize muffins on the table.

"Oh, he's into you." Shanny took a cinnamon muffin. "At least he was on Wednesday when he showed up at the bookstore, looking for you minutes after that robbery, right?"

Mari nodded. That was true. She couldn't deny the sexual attraction between them, though it was confusing. He didn't push her as so many men she'd dated had. And the other stuff he did made her heart ache when he did his withdrawing act, the way he'd stayed with her to search for Grandpa Connor, or the way he'd brought her a perfect Christmas tree. His kindness made it so puzzling when they ended Wednesday evening in separate cars without even a proper good-bye.

"You saw him Wednesday," Rachel prompted her.

Mari nodded. "He never even left the mall. He was waiting for me in the parking lot when I left my office." Maybe she didn't know where she stood with him, but maybe she wasn't totally deluded about his interest in her.

"What did you do? Where did you go?"

"We went to his parents' house. They've both passed away, but he still owns the house and an old family…friend keeps it in order."

"And?"

"We played a video game."

Her friends stared at her. "Wait. You? 'Sister' Maryrose, a video game?" Shanny was incredulous. "Your halo must be slipping."

"I know. It doesn't sound like me, but it wasn't about shooting or racing cars or stealing stuff. It's called *Rescue Force,* and Jack helped get it developed. It was strangely compelling and exhilarating."

"So, he just said, 'come on over and play a game'? That sounds like high school, like my parents aren't home so let's have sex," Rachel said. "How is the sex, by the way?"

"We haven't had…sex yet, just some hot…moments," Mari admitted. She didn't say how sweet, how almost adolescent the kisses were. "But the video game—it's what he does now—he's an investor behind this game. It's designed to retrain the brains of war-injured vets, to help them think flexibly. He wanted to show me."

"No sex? Are you okay with that?" Rachel reached for the muffin basket.

"I like not being rushed, and it's awkward that he's always got his security people around him."

"It's good that he's not rushing you, but is he hiding something?"

"That's what worries me," Mari admitted. "We have these really close moments, but I think he holds back because there's something he wants to tell me. It seems as if he's going to speak, and then he withdraws completely, just shuts down."

"Do you think he's on the spectrum? Personality disorder?" Shanny popped a bite of muffin in her mouth before she spoke again. "He's got the service dog, right?"

Rachel's brows lifted. "Service dog?"

"A black Lab named Soldier," Mari said. "Jack has a balance problem. He told me that."

"Does it have a name? Did you look it up?" Shanny asked, picking up her phone and thumbing in her password.

"I did not. Shanny, stop." Mari put her hand over Shanny's on the phone.

Their service person set their orders in front of them, and Rachel asked Shanny about her new man, Fletcher.

Shanny was genuinely happy. Fletcher appeared to be a solid guy. Mari picked at her omelet and moved the blueberries around on her plate, until she realized that Rachel was watching her.

"So how many times have you seen this Jack person?" Rachel asked.

"Since we met? Six." When she said it, it sounded like a lot, as if they were actually dating in some old-fashioned way. "The thing is that, half the times I've seen him, he just…withdraws, walks off…leaves."

"Like that day in the mall?" Shanny asked. "You told me he got a business call."

"I know," Mari admitted. "I didn't really see the pattern then."

"Mari." Rachel spoke in a no-nonsense voice. "Tell us what you do know about him. It will help you get your head clear."

Rachel was right. Mari put down her fork. Maybe saying the things that had been on an endless loop in her head would help.

"Okay. Here's what I know. He has a house on the Strand. He is very serious about security, and has a team of like…bodyguards around him. He went to Canyon."

"The exclusive boys prep school?" asked Shanny. "The one in the news with the scandal over the headmaster? On the Net, if you search 'bad headmasters,' he comes up—embezzling, grade tampering, affairs…"

"Shanny," said Rachel. "Still trying to get the story, here."

Mari continued. "I think he left home after high school, this place we went on Wednesday—"

"Nice place? Dump?" Shanny asked.

"Palace. Anyway, I'm guessing that he left for college, you know, normal stuff, but until Wednesday night, he had never gone back."

"Not normal," said Shanny. "*You* can't stay away from your family for a week. And you can't bring him to meet them. Not if he's got issues."

Rachel quelled Shanny with a glance and turned to Mari. "You mean that the first time he went home after years away, he brought you? Strikes me as pretty significant."

"But to play a video game? And no sex! That makes no sense," Shanny said.

"Sounds crazy, I know, but actually, I think the video game explains a lot," Mari said. "In the game, the player leads a team on a mission to rescue American hostages from militants. I think Jack is a rescued hostage. He has these tattoos on his neck that he tries to hide. I think they were put there by whoever took him, and I'm pretty sure that US Marines rescued him. I don't know why he was taken hostage in the first place."

"He hasn't told you? I wonder why not." Rachel spoke gently.

That was the trouble, the source of her doubts. Mari wanted him to tell her, to trust her. Whenever the conversation between them came close to that part of his past, he shut down. He was proud of the video game, though he hadn't wanted her to see the episode of the captives in the hut, and Mari didn't need a degree in psychology to understand that Jack feared her reaction to whatever part of his story explained how he got there.

Their server slid a black plastic tray with three separate checks onto the table. "Whenever, ladies," she said.

Shanny reached under the table and produced a square gold-foiled box. A sticky note on top read *In case of emergency, eat me.* "We thought you might need some serious chocolate to get you through the weekend."

"In case our wise counsel didn't help," added Rachel.

Mari laughed. Her friends knew her too well. "You two are the best."

A few minutes later, outside the restaurant, they exchanged hugs and prepared to plunge back into the world of retail.

Rachel offered Mari a final bit of encouragement. "One day at a time. If you don't stand in its way, Christmas will come. No Scrooges or Grinches or mysterious wounded boyfriends can stop it. So, eat your chocolate, find that Christmas spirit."

Chapter 14

By four on Saturday afternoon with no word from Jack, Mari was ready to crack open the gold box on her desk. It was time to admit that getting involved with him, however briefly, had been a mistake. She would have to return his shirts. She would have to decorate her tree alone.

She checked her messages. The fifth-grade chorus from Ocean View Elementary school was about to sing in front of Santa's workshop, and she hadn't heard back from the facilities crew about the audio system setup. It had been the kind of day that kept everyone running. She hoped that she could get some help with the big red plastic box of Santa hats she had for the kids. The box wasn't heavy, just awkward. She scooped up her phone and keys and went around her desk to check the large, color-coded calendar on her bulletin board for the director's name.

A sound behind her at her open door made her turn. Her dad stood there, giving her office an assessing once-over.

"Dad, hi," she said. He'd not been to her office before, and she wondered how he'd found her.

There wasn't much for him to see—beige walls, gray and tan carpet, desk with the big red box, laptop, and a houseplant; a small high-window that she'd been told was no good for escaping fires or active shooters; a fire extinguisher; a wall of flyers and notices to employees about California law, and of course, her bulletin board with its color-coded calendar of mall events. To a man who had worked on the ocean for most of his life, her office must have seemed claustrophobic.

"So this is where you spend your days," he said.

"Not really. Mostly, I'm out and about in the mall, working with people. I like it, you know. What are you doing here?" She moved to give him a hug. "I thought you hated malls."

"I do." He accepted her hug with a stiff, unbending posture, very different from their last hug at Thanksgiving. "Looks like you're in the middle of things."

"I am." She set her keys and phone next to the box on her desk. Maybe her dad could help her carry it. "Can you give me a minute to get this concert going?"

"Yeah, sure. I didn't want to call." He was dressed in a V-necked navy sweater over a white polo shirt and khakis. It was an outfit that passed for formal wear among her male relations.

"Looking sharp, Dad. Did you come to get something for Mom?" She resisted the temptation to glance at her watch.

He shifted to a wide-legged stance, his jaw tight. "I came to tell you something."

"Oh, that doesn't sound good." She had a sinking feeling.

He drew in a slow breath and let it out. "We've found a place that will take your grandfather."

"Take him?" Mari spoke over an instant lump in her throat. "You mean an assisted-living home?"

Her dad shoved his hands in his pockets. He looked almost angry. "He's way past that, Mari. It's a memory facility."

The lump in her throat hurt. She wanted to argue, to protest that Grandpa Connor belonged in his own place, that he needed his independence, needed his familiar surroundings. She thought of the locks Uncle Dan and Abby had installed the previous Saturday, of the neighbors she'd visited explaining how to contact the Lynch family if Connor wandered again. But the look on her dad's face stopped her. Maybe that look wasn't anger, maybe it was anguish too.

"Tell me the plan," she said.

"We're going to move him to Glenwood on Monday."

"Before Christmas?" Part of her mind went on thinking the conversation wasn't happening, but another part realized that this was no new plan. Desirable places had waiting lists. "How long has this move been in the works?"

Her dad looked away. "Your cousin Abby can't go on being Dad's sole caregiver, and the real estate agent says we've got a lot to do to get the house ready to put on the market."

He didn't say, but Mari understood. The sale of her grandfather's house would pay for his care. The only surprise was to her. She should have seen it coming, but still no one had mentioned the move at Thanksgiving. “When did the real estate agent come into the picture?”

“I don’t know. These things take time. He must have come on board a couple of weeks ago to see the house, and all.”

With sudden clarity, Mari knew exactly when, when Abby had ended Mari’s afternoon walks with Grandpa. Her dad, her uncle, and maybe even her mom had been showing the house to realtors and looking at places like this Glenwood. She knew it was their duty to make arrangements for a parent’s care. It couldn’t be easy either. It just hurt that no one had told her.

Her dad avoided her gaze. “Glenwood is on our side of the hill, so we can visit…whenever. You can see him when you come our way.”

Mari stood very still. The way he said “our” was a sharp reminder that her family had their side and their way, and she wasn’t part of it. They had seen her as an obstacle to their plan. They had felt it necessary to make arrangements behind her back. She’d been deliberately left out of the conversation. “Did my zip code mean no one was supposed to tell me?”

“We had to be able to do this, Mari, and let’s face it, you weren’t going to help the situation any.” He paused, not looking at her but at the red box on her desk. “Am I supposed to feel bad that he doesn’t get to play Santa Claus anymore? He never fit the part in my book, anyway, and now he doesn’t even know us.”

“We know him. That matters, doesn’t it?” She remembered the feel of her grandpa’s hand in hers the last time they’d walked together.

“Glenwood’s a good place,” her dad said. “Dad will be well cared for, and we will visit him.”

It wasn’t a rebuke, but it felt like one. For years it had been easy for her to visit her grandfather, and until he’d had his strokes, those visits had been full of talk and laughter and her grandpa’s wisdom. Maybe she’d been the selfish one. She blinked back the burn of oncoming tears.

“Well,” her dad said. He dug his car key out of his pocket. “I interrupted you. You’d best get back to your work.”

“Oh,” she said. The word was a reminder of what divided Mari and her family. It made her dad sound like a polite stranger. He wasn't even going to hug her good-bye. "Dad, I'm sorry if I sounded…doubtful. I was just surprised. I'm glad Grandpa Connor will be close to you."

He nodded. "We'll let you know when he's settled."

"Good." It wasn't the right word, but it was the only one she could manage. If her dad left now, he wouldn't see her cry. Her family was not the close family she imagined, and she was out of touch with them. She had believed there would be a Dickensian happy ending for them all, but it wasn't going to happen. They weren't going to forgive Grandpa Connor the way Scrooge's nephew forgave the old man. They were going to provide good care for him and dutifully visit him on their side of the hill. On the surface, her family's decision was the right one, but Mari felt an ache in her heart for the reconciliation that would never happen.

When she heard the door to the parking lot bang shut, she let the tears come until her face was a runny mess. Then she pulled a wad of tissues from her desk drawer. She wouldn't give up on her family yet. She would think the whole thing through later and have a talk with her mom, after the Ocean View Elementary School singers had their moment.

Mari blinked away the last of her tears and hefted the box of Santa hats. The large red plastic box made a kind of shield between her and the world, and she used her elbow to jab the light switch off as she left her office. The door closed behind her.

***

Jack's nausea was bad, but he needed to feel it, to remember who he was and why he was in the packed mall. The team had agreed to give him a second chance. The goal was full disclosure, and he wasn't going to wait for Mari in the safety of an SUV in the dark parking lot. He was going to meet her in her world, the ordinary world of buying and selling, a mall, that sterilized American version of a marketplace that attempted to banish the dirt and danger of real markets in other lands.

Even with Soldier at his side, he could not avoid being jostled by the Saturday crowd. From behind his dark glasses, he saw only restless, churning motion. He made it as far as a gingerbread cottage surrounded by a white picket fence and stands of snow-dusted artificial Christmas trees. Teenagers in green velveteen elf suits and belled caps directed children and their parents to a pair of tall toy soldiers stationed at the doors of the cottage. Red directional signs hung from a striped barber pole, pointing to Reindeer Parking and Santa's Workshop. Whatever Santa was up to inside the cottage, outside was an unmoving line of crying, wiggling kids and frazzled parents.

From the holiday schedule on the mall website, Jack knew that a children's singing group was scheduled to perform. It was the sort of event Mari handled. The young performers formed a semicircle facing the line of Santa visitors, but Jack saw no sign of Mari. The kids, looking to be ten or eleven years old, squirmed and poked at each other. Their director tapped the mic in his hand, but no sound emerged. Jack recognized the situation: a glitch in the sound system. He gripped the edge of a tall ceramic planter in the middle of the walkway and focused on the giant turkey on the other side of the open food court, still bobbing its head with a steady motion. His discomfort receded.

The singing group director left his mic in the hands of a serious-looking little girl in a white sweater, red plaid skirt, and shiny black shoes. He spoke to one of Santa's elves, but the elf, a dark-eyed teenager, simply shrugged her shoulders.

The director looked around as if someone in the crowd would come to his aid, and

Jack spotted Mari, hurrying toward the group, carrying a large red plastic box. She couldn't get her arms around the box or see over it. Her eyes had the glassy look of recent tears, but she offered the director a warm smile and her attention. He retrieved his mic and tried to restore order to his wiggling charges. Mari set the box at the foot of an artificial tree and slipped a hand in her jacket pocket, no doubt looking for a phone. Her face fell when she found nothing. She turned in a slow circle, her gaze sweeping the crowd. Then she squared her shoulders and headed around to the back of Santa's workshop. She never saw Jack.

Jack made eye contact with Bradley and followed Mari. She pushed aside a black curtain and slipped into a narrow space between the workshop and a store wall. Jack ordered Soldier to stay and slipped in after her. In the dim recess, he braced himself, flattening his palms on the walls on either side as he moved toward

Mari. The wall on his right was rough and cold. On his left the muffled sounds of Santa talking to his visitors came through the plywood back wall of Santa's workshop. Black rubber cord covers crisscrossed the floor, ending in massive plug strips against the wall.

Ahead of him, Mari dropped to her knees and began pushing plugs into outlets.

Jack reached her and leaned down, snagging her under one arm, and gently lifting. The softness of her arm in his hand made his head swim momentarily. She spun toward him, opening her mouth to protest.

"Jack," she said. Her pale face was even more tear-ravaged than he'd realized.

"What's wrong?"

She gave a shaky laugh. "What isn't? The mic's dead. The kids are ready to sing. I've locked myself out of my office without my phone. I can't get anyone from facilities to come, and I have no idea which one of these cords is the right one."

He brushed a thumb across her cheek below one makeup-smudged eye. "We can fix that. What made you cry?"

"Oh." She dropped her gaze from his, and for a moment she seemed to struggle to speak. "My grandpa."

"Wandering again?" he asked.

"No." She slipped her arm from his hold. "My family has decided to move him to a memory facility. But right now, I need—"

"—tech help? My guys can fix it." He touched the box at his waist and said a few words to Bradley. "Come on." He took her hand. "Let's get you out of here."

"Do I look that bad?" she asked.

"You have…black stuff…around your eyes."

"Oh." She glanced at the maze of cord covers on the floor. "You do know that chaos could erupt out there with frayed tempers, toddler meltdowns, and lots of grinchy behavior? It's my job to make this work."

"But not alone." He pivoted and pointed to Bradley standing at the opening of the narrow patch of flooring. Bradley flashed a light into the space, and Mari gave him a little wave. She looked one last time at the maze of cord covers and plugs and then brushed past Jack. The scent of her peppermint shampoo immobilized him for a heartbeat or two, then he caught up with her where the narrow passage opened back onto the mall. They stepped out, and Bradley ducked in.

As they came around from behind Santa's workshop, the ear-piercing screech of the mic coming on stopped the young singers from squirming. The director blew three notes on his pitch pipe; then he lifted his hands, his head nodding a beat.

Beside Jack, Mari held her breath. The next second, the young voices started singing about Dasher and Dancer and Comet and Vixen.

"Thank you," she said to Jack.

"Thank Bradley," he told her. "Later."

Jack let Mari lead him and Soldier across the food court and through a door marked Employees Only into an unoccupied room, blessedly quiet, no piped-in music. A quick glance gave Jack the layout—the center filled with round wood tables and molded black plastic chairs, illuminated by hanging globes of light. On either side of the room, dark gray doors were marked with restroom signage or with nameplates identifying official titles. At the far end was an exit to the parking lot, the door Mari had used on Wednesday. The room smelled of cold coffee.

"Which office is yours?" he asked.

She pointed to the nearest door on their right. "Is this when you pull out your credit card and do some magic trick with it?"

"Not exactly. No credit cards. Give me a moment." He left Soldier at her side and did a little reconnaissance, returning with a curved piece of a clear plastic food tub. He slid it down the slot between the door and jamb, disengaging the bolt from the striker plate. The door popped open.

The office was dark and smelled of her shampoo. Jack leaned against the wall next to the door while Mari retrieved her phone from the desk and sent some texts. Soldier curled up on the floor beside him.

She turned to him. "Thank you."

He waited for her to come closer. When she did, he reached out and pulled her up against him, closing his arms around her. She accepted his hold, resting her cheek against his chest. "Can you talk about your grandpa?"

"It's not what you think."

"What then?" he asked.

She didn't answer. He made himself wait, enjoying the rise and fall of her ribs against his. Usually he was the one who found it difficult to speak, to get the words out.

"I mean, I know Grandpa Connor is failing. And of course, my dad and my uncle are the ones to decide how best to care for him."

Jack waited some more. At last he heard her sigh.

"But when my dad came here today, he said things."

"What things?"

"I'm probably being unfair to him, to all of them, but they didn't want to tell me about their plans until it was all decided," she said. "I shouldn't mind. Moving Grandpa to a care facility wasn't my decision to make, but it felt…It felt as if they deliberately went behind my back, as if I'm not part of the family anymore."

He didn't change his hold on her. She still hadn't named the thing that had bothered her the most, the thing her dad said. Jack had been ignoring the fact that she had a family, thinking of her as being like him, alone in the world. He wanted to keep her alone with him. But her family mattered to her. The hurt they'd inflicted came through in the thickness of her voice.

"My dad made me understand what my family really thinks about what I do and how I live. I know retail isn't some noble profession. It's not like law or medicine or nursing or running a center for underserved kids, like your friend Huntington. What I do is help people shop, buy things—silly stuff, useful stuff, ugly sweaters, flowers, books, pots and pans, gifts, sometimes stuff they don't need. I want them to have fun shopping, even if they don't always behave well. And they don't. Even at Christmas." She laughed. "Maybe especially at Christmas. Entitled customers tell clerks making minimum wage how important they are because they make hundreds of dollars an hour. People fight over parking places. I'm ranting, aren't I? I'll stop now."

"I don't want you to stop." He was pretty sure he could go on holding her for hours in the dark, her arms around him, her cheek against his chest, her breath coming in warm, soft gusts as she spoke. The ache of sexual longing was there, but next to it was another ache that he couldn't locate in any specific body part.

"I shouldn't care what my family thinks of retail. Coast Plaza is just a mall, just a place to go shopping. If some developer bulldozed it next week, the world would go on. It wouldn't be like the burning of the great library in Alexandria."

She spoke with affection for the ordinary, familiar world of which she was a part, a world worth protecting because it contained her. She knew its flaws, but she loved it anyway.

"I should apologize to you," she said.

"I don't think so."

"No, really, I should." She pulled back in his arms, looking up at him, her eyes big in the dark. And he held himself very still to keep from kissing her. "My grandpa's agitation in the last month probably had nothing to do with your fortress house and everything to do with real estate agents coming into his bungalow. He must have known that change was coming, and he must have felt so helpless."

She leaned her head against his chest. He wanted to keep her there, just like that, trusting him, believing him to be a good man, comforted by his arms around her. He didn't want what was coming next, but it would come whether he wanted it or not.

"Why are you here?" she asked.

"I have something for you," he said. That was true, even if it was a partial evasion, one more delay in revealing his true self to her. He did want her to have one thing from Paloma's box. As soon as he'd seen it, he'd wanted Mari to have it.

"You know, we're not even 'together,' and I was thinking of breaking up with you," she said. "Then you show up and help me. It's what you do."

"Don't think of me as any kind of hero." The words sounded harsh in his own ears. His plan to tell her who he really was looked selfish. Even his motive for telling her the truth was selfish. He wanted to have sex with her. He'd wanted sex from the day he'd first started watching her walk the old man along the Strand.

"Are you going to tell me you've done terrible things?"

"Something like that."

"Tell me." Her voice was firm, demanding to face whatever blow was coming.

There were ways to tell the story to make himself look good, or less bad, but he was going to put it as plainly as he could. "In other parts of the world, the lawless, unstable parts, businesses and organizations like the UN need private security to protect them, and private security firms hire consultants like me to help them obtain the weapons and technology they need. That's what I did when I left college. I made myself a weapons expert and was well paid for my expertise. I met buyers and consulted with them wherever weapons deals were made, places like Tashkent and Abu Dhabi."

She didn't speak, but he could feel the change in her, the stiff wariness.

"I made it a rule to check out my clients to make sure they had contracts with legitimate businesses. But the truth is, weapons have a way of getting into the wrong hands. Schoolgirls get kidnapped. Boys are forced to become soldiers. Villages are emptied. I didn't think of those things. I thought that by following the rules, I was not to blame for what I saw around me. I was arrogant. I thought I knew who I was dealing with, but I didn't."

He was coming to the hard part now. "So, I got conned. I made a deal for a party that was a front. The weapons ended up in the hands of brutal militants. Young soldiers were sent to recover those weapons. It was supposed to be routine. Part of Operation Bulldog Bite, it was called. They met extraordinary firepower.

"But I wasn't done being arrogant. It took me awhile to discover the true identity behind the front man. Then I went after him, and he sent militants for me in a marketplace. More people died, ordinary people, villagers buying their bread and cheese curds. I don't know their names. I was captured and held. Later, two US Marines died getting me out of captivity."

"And the front man? Did you stop him?"

"No. He's still out there."

She shuddered in his arms, and he released her. She stepped back to look at him. He saw that she assessed him differently now. She might see his visible wounds, the tattoos on his neck, and remember the burn marks on his ribs, but now she knew the guilt he bore, his responsibility for the blood of others in the dust of that market.

"Thank you for telling me." She didn't say that his words had changed everything. She didn't have to. No good-bye was needed.

Simultaneously, the phone on her desk buzzed, and the doors to the employee room flew open. She reached for her phone, but when someone called to her from the community room, she let the phone go to message.

"Mari, you there? Where do you want this box of Santa hats to go?" Mari stepped out of her office into the larger room. Laughter and greetings filled the room beyond her office as her work world claimed her. Jack remained in the dark and the quiet.

He straightened away from the wall and steadied himself briefly, then he touched the box at his waist and got an answering buzz. Soldier came to immediate attention. Jack reached down and opened the pack on Soldier's harness, then retrieved a newspaper-wrapped item and placed it on her desk.

In the community room outside of her office, as Santa removed his red hat and coat, three elves still in their green velveteen suits snacked and texted. A Latino man in a mall uniform engaged Mari in conversation, and Jack passed behind her out into the darkness of the parking lot. The guys were waiting.

"Mission accomplished," he said as he swung himself up into the SUV.

Chapter 15

After a few words with Santa and his elves, Mari extracted herself from the happy group in the employee community room. She managed one last smile for Elena, the teenage elf, and returned to her office. Of course, Jack was gone.

A small, newspaper-wrapped package sealed with clear tape lay on her desk. Jack said he had something for her. She knew what it was: a parting gift. He'd said his piece and walked away again, his way of telling her that they came from different worlds and didn't belong together. How ironic that she thought she would have to break it off with Jack when he'd been planning to end it himself. The little gift was proof of that.

Her office was suddenly claustrophobic. First her dad and then Jack had dropped their bombshells on her. Her chest hurt. Emotion crowded the office, and Mari needed out. She texted Shanny, tucked away her laptop, shrugged into her coat, and grabbed her purse and keys. She snatched up Jack's gift and shoved it into her coat pocket. She would face whatever was inside later, at home. Her phone pinged with Shanny's return text. And, like that, Mari had a place to go. On her phone, she booked a ride to the old Fireside Tavern.

***

As soon as she entered the tavern, she knew it was the perfect place to banish thoughts of Jack. People stood or sat, jammed elbow to elbow in the long narrow space, the holiday mood evident in their laughter and raised voices. Above the bar, tacky red balls hung from strands of silver tinsel. Pop versions of seasonal songs added another blaring layer of sound. The movement of bodies stirred air filled with beer and sweat, perfume and the occasional hint of cigarette smoke. Jack wouldn't last five minutes in such a place.

Shanny waved Mari over to join a group standing around two tall tables against the wall opposite the bar. Fletcher, Shanny's new man, had one arm draped over her shoulders and gestured, beer in hand, with the other. Mari was introduced, and a cute guy named Tim, a high school soccer coach, volunteered to get her a drink. Within minutes, Mari had a glass of dark, malty Irish stout in hand. She flashed Tim a smile and prepared to laugh her way back to planet happy.

For half an hour or more, the conversation was of football and the playoffs. Then the talk turned to how 2015's toys weren't like the ones they'd all had to have for Christmas in the 90s. The men were divided on which of the old-style game controllers they'd wanted back then, but agreed on their favorite movie action figure. The women in the group debated the merits of popular doll franchises. Mari had an instant memory of wanting one of the big expensive dolls that came with names and histories, outfits and accessories. Her dream doll had been the one with Swedish immigrant ancestry. That year, their eighth year, Mari and Shanny planned for their dolls to be twins, but on Christmas Day only Shanny received the longed-for doll. Mari received a Barbie.

The recollection snapped the pieces of her family's history together. Now she understood. There had been no expensive gifts that year because that was the year when her Grandpa Connor landed in jail, and the boat, her family's livelihood, was lost. No wonder her dad couldn't see her grandpa as Santa. For a moment the buzz in the bar disoriented her, and she put her glass down on the table. At her side, Tim noticed and asked if she wanted to step outside. She shook her head.

She stayed until her cheek muscles hurt from smiling. Tim offered to drive her home, but she opted for a ride from her phone app. When she opened her apartment door, the smell of real Christmas tree hit her, and she silently cursed Jack for invading her space, her office, her apartment, her head, her heart. She dragged herself up the stairs to the living room and sank down on the loveseat that faced the tree, illuminated only by dim lights from the alley.

Jack had chosen the classic male breakup strategy. She knew it from dozens of tear-soaked, girl-talk sessions ever since middle school. It was what guys, men, did. They told some girl or woman that she wasn't at fault in the relationship, that the flaw was in them. *It's not you, babe, it's me*—that was the line. *I must break up with you because I'm some kind of jerk. Or because I have some promise to keep.* Men liked to call that honor and duty.

And Jack was more than a jerk. She had been shocked by his revelations. She'd known from the beginning that some terrible thing haunted his past, but she'd never suspected that he'd done so much harm in the world. He was no nice guy, like Tim the soccer coach. Jack admitted that he'd pocketed money for helping enemies acquire weapons. She understood what he didn't say. Maybe he'd been a hostage somewhere like the characters in his video game, but mostly he'd operated in places away from the blood and the dying. And he wasn't free of the things he'd done. She guessed that the promise he meant to fulfill had to do with the man who'd tricked him. Maybe it had to do with justice, but—a chill went through her—it sounded like revenge.

She pulled his package from her coat pocket and held it in her lap, pressing her thumbs to the stiff, irregular shape. She should toss it. She'd thought she was beginning to understand him. How wrong she'd been. Another sign that her judgment about men was off. She'd mistaken her grandpa's character, for heaven's sake. Really, she was laughable. She had a fleeting thought that she needed a complete career change. Maybe to the tech sector, to some position in which decisions depended entirely on algorithms, not people sense.

Her thoughts returned to the little package. The awkwardness of the wrapping was so like him that it stopped her for a long moment.

Then she peeled away the tape and newsprint to find a whimsical carved wooden Santa about four inches tall. He was old and a bit battered with nicks in his cuffs and black boots. He had rosy cheeks, gold trim on his hat, and a long, red Santa coat faded to the color of old bricks. His eyes were bright with a look of perpetual surprise in a pink-cheeked face above a white beard curved like a sliver of new moon. Tiny gold stars dangled from his hands and the pointed tip of his cap. She might not understand Jack Ryker, but he understood her.

Her chest ached. Her eyes stung. She swallowed another lump in her throat. The old Santa must have come from the box his nanny Paloma had wanted him to have, from his life before he became a hardened man, one who'd left a nasty, dangerous business only when a deal gone wrong revealed the real cost of the arms trade.

Once there had been a boy who'd believed in Santa, in goodness and generosity. That boy no longer existed. She could mourn him and his lost innocence and what might have been possible between them, but she and he belonged to different worlds. Mari pushed up off the loveseat and crossed to the tree. She found a hook, attached it to the Santa's cap, and hung him from a branch.

***

Once Jack stopped looking for Mari out his window, he realized that the perfect place to trap Evans had been staring him in the face for weeks—the old cement pier, a place where Evans could move freely, carry a knife, and dispose of the weapon in the sea. Evans was no marksman, and even if he had found a new accomplice as a shooter since the Grindstone concert in the spring, the length of the pier plus the wide beach and the prevailing onshore wind would make a shot from even the nearest rooftop difficult.

On Friday afternoon from the pier's midpoint, Jack looked out toward the hills of the Palos Verdes peninsula, the southern end of the vast Santa Monica Bay. The stiff ocean breeze blew his hair around his face and plastered his board shorts against his legs. The winter season crowd was thin along the pier's 928-foot length, with maybe fifty people strung between the lifeguard tower at the beach end and the round Mediterranean-style concession stand at the ocean end. The concession stand was closed, and only a few fishermen leaned against the pier railing, trying for surf perch, croakers, and small rays in the surging gray-blue waters below. The pier stood high enough above the water that a man would think twice before jumping off, which meant that if Evans followed Jack out onto the pier, whatever happened in their encounter, the team could block Evans' escape.

The only surveillance on the pier was near the concession stand, but Jack wore a bodycam. A bit of Evans's DNA was the evidence Jack needed to link Evans conclusively to weapons used against US troops. With his many aliases, no one had yet linked the man to illegal arms deals, but Jack knew it could be done. At some point in his career, Evans had crossed a line and begun selling arms to security units involved in actions against civilians. From there, apparently, Evans had stopped drawing any lines at all in his dealings. An enormous biometric military database kept track of iris scans and DNA, and fingerprints that had appeared on various weapons and bomb fragments in Afghanistan. Jack knew that Evans's prints were in the system on stuff no loyal American should ever have touched, ordnance that had killed US soldiers.

Huntington had said Jack was predictable, so that's what he'd been all week. He had created a new normal for himself, walking the length of the pier and back every day at the same time, just after lunch, when the crowd was lightest, first with Cole, and then alone. He stopped in the same places each time, on each side of the pier, so he was visible from the shore. One benefit of his cancelled effort to win Mari's affection was his improved ability to walk. He'd spent almost no time in his chair for a week or in his bed, for that matter. He couldn't lie in bed and not think of her, and he couldn't look down at the churning surface of the waves below without getting dizzy, but he could manage the walk. He would expose himself as a target as long as it took to tempt Evans to act.

Jack had plenty of backup. The guys were speaking to him again, and they liked the new plan. Soldier stood beside him, and on the pier's opposite side, closer to the ocean end, Rashaad hung over the rail, rod in hand, in the guise of a fisherman. They'd even had fish tacos Wednesday night from a bonito he'd caught. Going back to an aerial map of the neighborhood, the team had rechecked real estate deals, app-driven rentals, and changes in occupancy around Jack's fortress. They found three places near the pier where Evans had likely holed up recently. When he moved again, they'd be on to him. Bradley had reached Agent Arias, and Arias had agreed to send the FBI to any place Evans left for possible DNA. Now, it was only a matter of Evans deciding when to strike. One of these days, he would. Jack just had to have more patience than his enemy.

Jack let the wind buffet him as he waited for Bradley's signal from the shore where the rest of the team waited and watched. When the signal came, Jack pivoted to face the Strand. A flash of light glinting off a window instantly caught him in the eyes. Even with dark glasses, the light made him pause to steady himself. Soldier moved into position to brace him. The dancing light moved off his face. It was a good sign, a sign that Evans was watching and waiting.

***

Late Saturday, Josh Huntington crossed the rain-soaked parking lot headed for the mall's south entrance. He was taking Emma and Max for Max's first ever visit to Santa, and he wanted to keep things cool because he didn't know how Emma really felt about taking her kid to see Santa. In the Rover, she'd been unusually quiet. Josh knew she wasn't used to sharing parenting decisions. She'd been a single mom for six years. He had to be ready to pull the plug if she changed her mind.

Earlier as they piled into the Rover, Max had solemnly assured Josh that he knew the mall Santa was a pretend Santa. Max was Emma's kid, after all, a realist to the core, but for a realist, he seemed pretty excited. The heels of the kid's rain boots flashed green light as he stomped through puddles in the parking lot, walked on curbs, and generally ricocheted around Josh and Emma. At the mall entrance, Josh sneaked a peek to see how Emma was handling Max's obvious exuberance.

Santa visits were more organized than Josh remembered from his childhood. He'd used a phone app to make a reservation for them in the last afternoon time slot. They'd chosen it because the Canyon School C-Notes, the boys *a capella* group, would be singing. The group included Ulysses, aka The Bookman, a kid from the center where Josh now worked, and Ulysses's friend Tyler. Josh, who had been a C-Note in his time at Canyon, had helped the boys get their harmonizing down. A group of kids from the Center, where Josh now worked, would be there to see The Bookman, and Will Sloan and his wife, the former Annie James, were coming, too. The whole gang was going for pizza afterward, generally another Emma no-no.

When they entered the mall, Emma spotted the flower shop and ducked in to admire its display of Christmas trees. Josh stopped to text Ryker to join them later, but got no reply. Inviting Ryker places was like inviting Scrooge. He hoped the guy would join them for Christmas Eve at Mae Sloan's. He had the picture of Ryker and the puppy on his phone, and he'd been tempted to send it to Mari Lynch, until Emma told him to stop matchmaking. Josh still wanted to show the picture to Mari. With any luck, they'd run into her. Max tugged Josh's hand, and Josh put away his phone.

"You know how *this* Santa's not the *real* Santa?" Max asked.

"Uh-huh."

"But we can't say so because, to little kids, he is real."

"Uh-huh."

"Which might be like a lie, except it's not." Max swung their joined hands back and forth.

"Explain, buddy."

"Well, the guy in the mall is like…pretending. The real Santa's a person in a story, sort of an idea. Mom would call him a 'concept.'"

Josh never failed to be astonished at how Max picked up words. "Interesting. And what kind of concept is Santa?"

"The good kind. Santa is this idea that people should care about kids, all the kids in the world, with no kids left out, and try to give them things to make them happy. That's why I like Santa."

Once again, Josh had to admire Emma's parenting and his luck. Not every guy had a kid like Max pick him to be his dad.

Emma emerged from the flower shop with a small red-tissue-paper-filled bag over one wrist. Josh raised an eyebrow. Without his trust fund, they were watching their pennies.

"Just a little something for our tree," she said. She turned to Max. "Ready to meet Santa?"

"Sure, Mom. I'm just going to say hi to him and tell him that my mom knows what I want, so no worries." Emma flashed Josh a grin, and he knew she was okay with the plan.

Max let go of Josh's hand and spun in a circle. "And we're going to hear the singers, aren't we? The Bookman and Tyler?"

***

Jack stood in the shower after the day's afternoon pier walk. Today's effort to lure Evans out of hiding had been worse than useless. A gusty rain squall had soaked him to the skin out on the deserted pier, where only a few hardy souls had braved the sharp wind. There'd been no sign of Evans. Evans liked crowds and knives. Returning, Jack had fallen on a slick patch of cement and banged his right knee. The shower washed away the blood and grit, but the knee throbbed. He cut off the water and stood in the warm steam.

Someone pounded on the bathroom door, and Soldier barked a single, sharp alert bark. Jack wrapped himself in a towel and opened the door to Bradley's grim face.

"Kitchen, now," Bradley said.

Jack followed. The guys were all there around the kitchen table except Miguel, who had perimeter duty. Spread out on the big table lay five small black-and-white photos of Mari Lynch—at lunch in the food court, getting into her car, talking with her friend Shanny outside the bookstore, exiting the building, and surrounded by elves outside Santa's workshop. The pictures bore time stamps from the mall's security cameras. None of the pictures included Jack or the times he'd met with Mari, but Jack knew from the grim faces around the table that the pictures were Evans' work.

"How? When?" He tapped the nearest picture. He had to know the worst. The pictures were a clear threat, not to Jack this time, but to Mari. Evans had changed his tactics.

"In this." Bradley held up the gray plastic sleeve of a newspaper, and the paper itself. "We've got footage. A kid on a bike tossed it into the yard at 1530 hours."

Jack entered a blank space, the complete absence of thought, only a silent howl filling his head. He thought they'd been careful. There had been no sign of Evans any of the times they'd been together after that meeting in the food court, and the team had been sure that those photos had not captured Mari's face.

He thought he'd learned humility. His body was next to useless. It could betray him at any time. He wasn't going to bring Evans down with fighting skill; that was for his team, warriors all. But he knew looking at the pictures of Mari on the table that there was a deeper level of humility he'd failed to reach. He'd believed in his mental superiority over Evans. He'd been sure that he could control the time and place of their encounter. Instead, Evans had chosen the place to test Jack; Evans had set the cost of failure.

Jack's vision narrowed. Nothing had changed. Everything had changed. When he'd decided to go after and expose Evans, Jack had unleashed a monster, and the monster had followed him home. It didn't matter how Evans had discovered the link between Jack and Mari. All that mattered was that once again Evans had chosen a battlefield where innocents would suffer for any misstep of Jack's, this time not nameless villagers in a distant highland valley, this time the one person Jack knew with blinding certainty he...loved. He rested his fingertips on the picture of Mari exiting the mall. She was completely vulnerable. She had no idea Evans existed. Jack hadn't told her.

His mind speeded up, searching for ways to protect her. The pictures told him that Evans had access to mall security systems. It was likely that he could monitor communications among the security people. No point in calling them while Evans listened in. The local police weren't in the loop.

"You called Agent Arias?" he asked Bradley.

"The FBI is on the way."

He needed to get to Mari. Now. "Two-minute drill," he said. They'd practiced the two-minute drill many times. It meant that his team could be under way in less than two. He pivoted away from the table, but Nick grabbed his arm.

"Don't go. It's a friggin' trap. Evans is leading you around by the dick." Nick swore. "As long as she doesn't know who he is, she's okay, right?" Nick pointed at the food court picture full of people in the background behind Mari. "What are we effing going to do in a mall? There are collaterals everywhere."

Nick was right. The situation sucked, but Jack looked at the men around him. They were ready. They wanted this crack at Evans, wanted to put him out of action.

"*We*," Rashaad said, putting a hand on Nick's shoulder and fixing a grim gaze on Jack, "go now. Move."

Jack gave a thumbs-up. In stride, he told Bradley to find Mari first. He wanted his team around her in ten minutes. He reminded himself that he was Evans's target, and he hoped that Nick was right, that as long as Evans didn't reveal himself to Mari, as long as she didn't know who Evans was, he wouldn't hurt her. But with Evans, no one was safe.

Chapter 16

Mari set the big red box of Santa hats on one end of the volunteer gift-wrap table in front of the bookstore. The volunteers had left for the day, and she gathered the boys from the C-Notes singing group around her to distribute hats. She was operating in a semi-fog since she'd last seen Jack, but she smiled and said the right thing and no one seemed to notice, except Shanny and Rachel, and Mari was keeping away from them.

In their preppy, blue, untucked shirts, blue-and-gold school ties, and khakis, the boys looked absurdly young to her, like puppies. They accepted hats and tried them on at rakish angles, full of happy energy, singing snatches of melody and harmonizing spontaneously. Their plan was to sing for the visitors in line at Santa's workshop and then take their show down the mall's main aisle, stopping to perform along the way. Mari had made sure there would be no mic trouble for them by having Omar, the mall's facilities head, check those plug strips earlier.

She was putting the lid on the hat box when she became aware of a man beside her standing a little too close. She shifted to face him and get some space.

"Excuse me, miss," he said. "Are you in charge here?"

"How can I help you?" She didn't recognize him as one of the volunteers. He had a pleasant face with a curly wave of light brown hair across his forehead, probably someone she'd forgotten in her post-Jack fog.

"Not me," he said. "It's just that I noticed an elderly—"

"*Mari*," someone shouted, and she turned toward the new voice, but the crackle of a mall security walkie-talkie stopped her. It had come from the man at her side. She glanced back, but he was walking away. She stared after him, puzzled. She didn't think he was a new hire. He wasn't wearing a mall employee shirt or jacket, so it didn't make sense that he had a walkie-talkie, but that's what she'd heard. She knew the sound. The brief interaction felt wrong, the way he'd stood too close, the odd question, and the walkie-talkie. As she watched, the crowd swallowed him up.

She shoved the box of hats under the table. The bare folding table looked a little tacky without its wrapping paper, but Omar would be back soon to put it and the hats away.

She heard her name again, and saw Josh Huntington wave from the line of Santa visitors.

***

Jack swung himself down from the SUV outside the mall's south entrance, and Nick stepped up and adjusted a tiny body cam on the collar of Jack's black sweater.

"You don't let Evans off you. You don't let him go. He belongs to us," Nick said. Nick was right. The plan had always been for Jack to be the bait. He was no trained warrior.

Jack turned to Bradley. "Signal me the minute you have her safe."

"Here, take this." Nick thrust a Santa hat at Jack.

"Where'd you get this?"

"Your box of old stuff. Wear it. If things go south, we can spot you. You're a hemorrhoid, man, but you're our hemorrhoid. Got it?"

Jack put on the hat, then entered the mall and headed for the main aisle. *First things first. Lead Evans away from Mari.* Jack needed to slow everything down, to give his team time to get into place, for Bradley to reach Mari, and Rashaad to start down from the other end of the mall with Soldier.

Jack's strategy was to break the long walk into short segments, no more than ten yards at a time, like the lines on a football field, or the individual frames of a movie. Where the entry met the main aisle, he stopped next to a kiosk displaying cell phone covers. To his right, a bell ringer collected donations in a hanging pot. Jack took a few seconds to fix the image of the mall layout in his brain again, a maze of openings and interlocking passages.

The whole setting was against him—the dizziness-inducing welter of sound and light, his stomach-churning fear for Mari, and his ugly memories of that other marketplace. Jack reasoned that

Evans picked the mall to seize the advantage, but a man's sense of advantage could also make him careless. Jack wouldn't forget that.

He was as ready as he was going to be. Under his sweater, he wore a light Kevlar vest. The black box at his waist connected him to his team. They could send encrypted messages that Evans could neither hack nor detect. If all else failed, Rashaad and Soldier, coming from the mall's north end, could find Jack anywhere.

He started down the wide central walkway, keeping to the right, stopping for each of the security cameras. His plan was simple—get Evans out of the building by offering him what he wanted—access to Jack—and once he had Evans away from innocent people, stay alive long enough for his team to find them. Ahead of him several yards away were two narrow openings between the shops. Both led to the back parking lot, and either one would serve his purpose.

The place was packed. A thousand impressions swarmed his senses and waves of dizziness washed over him. He moved with a slight hitch in his stride from the banged knee, and his stomach lurched with each unbalanced step. Evans would emerge from the thick of the crowd, counting on human shields to protect him. He'd likely come at Jack from the side and to the rear, out of Jack's peripheral vision. Jack caught some looks as he passed people with his halting stride. With any luck someone would call mall security to report a suspicious character impersonating Santa. Evans might be monitoring security broadcasts, but he wouldn't want armed responders investigating his activities.

Jack fixed his attention on the first exit to the parking lot. It opened off the main aisle just beyond the cookware store ahead on Jack's right. His team should be in place. They should have Mari safe by now, but the black box at his waist remained silent. The familiar signs of his imbalance, the cold sweat and faint nausea, arrived. He slowed to a mere shuffle of movement, concentrating on his breathing.

As he neared the store, the smell of hot cider stopped him. A woman in a bright green apron offered tiny paper cups to customers at the entrance with its open double doors. He made himself look for a still point in the churning movement around him. Beyond the cookware store, the main walkway angled left, leading in another thirty yards or so to Santa's workshop. He could see the bookstore where Mari's friend worked. There was a long empty table in front, off to one side, and beyond the table, the black curtain concealing the electrical outlets for Santa's workshop. A line of waiting parents and kids stretched around the fenced off workshop. Jack made himself move. He saw no sign of Bradley or Rashaad.

Instead, he saw Mari. A bunch of teenagers wearing Santa hats milled around her, and there were Huntington and Emma and her kid Max. Sloan and his wife, Annie, with her unmistakable red hair and distinct baby bump joined the group. The teenagers in the Santa hats began to form two curved lines facing Santa's workshop, and Jack realized who they were: the Canyon boys' singing group.

For a disorienting moment, he was back in time, reminded of Canyon where his journey to this moment had started, where he and Sloan had been the dark outsiders while Huntington was the golden boy. A memory flashed of the night he stood outside the headmaster's office in the dark, seeing through the blinds, a woman with red hair. He understood that moment now, how it had misled him and fueled his anger, led to all the mistakes that had brought him to this time and place, including the biggest one: unleashing Evans.

Everything else fell away, and he was left with what mattered most, with who he truly was. He was the man who was supposed to love those friends. And love Mari Lynch. She looked subdued and unhappy in spite of a small glittering green Christmas tree on the front of her black T-shirt.

His gut spasmed. His head buzzed as if someone had turned on a fluorescent light in his brain. He couldn't take another step. Evans must be close, watching, and Jack's guys were nowhere to be seen. Jack struggled to quiet the noise in his head.

***

"Hey, Mari," Josh Huntington said. "Thanks again for giving the C-Notes a chance to sing down here in the South Bay. It means their local fans can see them."

Mari nodded. Her smile had pretty much frozen in place, and she hoped no one noticed. She had told herself she was doing fine, but surrounded by Jack's friends, glimpsing what might have been, unable to correct his friends' assumptions of where things stood between herself and Jack, she was not fine.

She was pathetic, unable to stop the rush of thoughts of him. A black service dog, in harness, walking with another man, looked like Jack's Soldier, but of course, the man with the dog wasn't Jack. Still, the dark-skinned man had a distinctly military bearing, an earbud, and a suspicious bulge under his shirt at the waistline. Another "something's-not-right" twinge tightened her gut.

"Hey." Max, the little blond boy at Huntington's side, shouted and pointed at the dog. "That's Jack's dog. That's Soldier. I know him. Can I pet him?" He ducked under the velvet cord separating the Santa visit line from general mall traffic. Huntington's hand shot out and grabbed his shoulder. "Hold it, Max. Looks like Soldier's working."

A quick exchange of concerned looks between Huntington and Jack's other friend, Sloan, tightened the knot of tension in Mari's gut. The dog *was* Soldier, and Jack's friends didn't like the idea of Jack without the dog. The man with Soldier stopped and turned aside as if absorbed by the display in a shop window.

She looked around, trying to spot Jack in the shifting crowd, and saw only moms and dads, little kids and teens, grandmas and grandpas. Really, she had to get a grip. Uneasiness was turning her into a Shanny: looking for disaster instead of enjoying the season with the people around her. She moved to find a place in the audience and tried to focus on the young singers.

But she couldn't stop her uneasy gaze from wandering. From her new spot, she glanced south down the mall, and a Santa hat caught her eye, a still point in the moving crowd. For a moment, she thought it was one of the Canyon boys, then she realized the man in the hat was Jack. He stood immobile, no dark glasses, just an agonized expression on his face. Their gazes met, and his whole concentration was on her. She thought she'd never truly seen him until now, never understood his locked loneliness or why he did the things he did.

As she stared, the man from before, the man with the wave of light brown hair over his forehead came up on Jack from behind. The man put his hand on Jack's shoulder and said something. Jack's gaze shifted away from Mari, but not before the other man looked her way and caught her staring. The glint of malice in his eyes made her gasp.

Abruptly, the man swung Jack around. Mari couldn't be sure, but she thought Jack's hand clawed at the man's neck. She started forward. Then Bradley was at her side, taking her arm. “Ms. Lynch,” he said. “A word.” He turned her away from Jack. “Stay with me, please. We’ve got a situation here.”

“Jack’s in trouble,” she said. “*Danger*,” she amended. “He’s in danger.” Looking at Bradley’s closed face, she realized Jack had always been in danger. He wasn’t just some reclusive eccentric with an entourage.

“We’re handling it,” Bradley said. “Come with me.”

Behind them, the C-Notes began to sing an old Southern California favorite about the little Saint Nick. Mari refused to budge. “Stop. Tell me what’s happening. Where is that man taking Jack?”

“What man?” Bradley whipped his head around, scanning the main aisle.

“He has a wave of light brown hair over his forehead.”

“You saw him?” Turning back to her, Bradley gave her arm a shake. “Did he see that you saw him?”

“Yes.”

In her ear Bradley swore violently.

Chapter 17

"You've screwed everything up, Ryker." Evans squeezed Jack's nape. "You know better. Your girlfriend will pay."

Jack's stomach contracted painfully. His vision blurred. He struggled to get a breath as the sharp tip of a knife angled up against his right side under the edge of his vest. With each step, the knife cut deeper. The box at his waist vibrated. When he touched it, Evans swore and pulled the knife from Jack's side. Evans clawed at the box, pulling it free of Jack's belt.

When Evans glanced at the object in his hand, Jack pivoted, swinging out of Evans's grip. He staggered toward the cookware shop. At the entrance, his wounded knee gave, and he went down, catching himself with his hands. The green-aproned lady rushed to his side. Around him voices murmured, asking what happened, what's going on? People passed between them and Evans.

"Bad knee," he said, making an effort to grin, as if he were some weekend warrior with a sports injury. He couldn't see where Evans had gone. Without the box, Jack couldn't reach his team.

"Let me call security," the aproned lady said. "They have carts, you know, if you need to get to first aid."

"No need. Thanks," he told her. He reached for the handle of the open door and pulled himself up. He kept his back to the woman and a smile in place as he edged into the store. He put his hand to his side and applied pressure to the knife wound. He could smell blood.

***

Standing where she'd last seen Jack, Mari refused to budge as she tried to ignore Bradley's hold on her arm. She tried to picture exactly where Jack had been when the man grabbed him. She thought he had been standing between the baby clothes store and a group of shimmering silver Christmas trees in the center of the passageway.

She wanted to shout for everyone to stop, to stand still. Jack's Santa hat should be visible, but the big main aisle of the mall was a mass of bobbing heads, as indistinguishable as one wave from another in a choppy sea. It occurred to her that the mall was always like a choppy sea for Jack.

Beside her, Bradley and Huntington spoke in low voices.

"Is this guy armed?" Huntington asked.

"He likes knives," Bradley said.

"Do you need more manpower? Mall security? Police?" Huntington persisted, his voice strained.

Bradley tugged her arm, but Mari needed time to think. This was not a drill. It was not happening somewhere else. She turned to Huntington. "Keep everyone safe," she said. "The man who took Jack has a mall walkie-talkie. He'll hear anything security says."

"You saw him?" Huntington's expression was somber. Behind them, where the Santa line wound around a white picket fence, people cajoled and scolded their children into waiting.

Mari nodded, still trying to fix the spot she'd last seen Jack. *Next to an emergency exit*, she thought. Had he slipped out of the mall? "Do you have someone in the parking lot?" she asked Bradley.

"We'll protect Ryker. Let us do our job," Bradley said.

"But you've lost him, haven't you," she argued.

Bradley's cinder block face didn't change. "First, we have to hide you, miss. This man is going to come after you."

"Because I saw him?"

Bradley made no answer. He put his bulk between Mari and her view down the mall. The boys from the Canyon singing group finished their first number to enthusiastic applause. Two boys came to the front, one dark-skinned and dark-haired wearing tinted shades, one fair and blond. The boys snapped their fingers in a synchronized rhythm and began a new number. More people stopped and gathered to listen. Under cover of the crowd, Bradley pulled Mari along the fence surrounding Santa's workshop until they reached the narrow passage that concealed the plug strips. He shoved her into the dim space.

As hiding places went, it was definitely handy, but there was no back door, no way out except past Bradley's considerable bulk. Adrenaline pumped through Mari, making her shake, her nerves screaming for action. Jack was out there alone with knife man, and Bradley, big, immovable Bradley, wasn't letting go of her arm.

"Who is he?" she asked Bradley, her voice shaking. "Why did he take Jack?"

He didn't answer. Instead he posted himself at the entrance to the enclosure, listening to whatever his colleagues had to say over their wire.

Mari leaned against the wall, saying nothing, trying to see past Bradley. Whoever Jack's assailant was, he was the reason for all the crazy driving and the super security around Jack. She wanted answers. She wanted to know what Jack was up against. She needed to get her shaking voice under control. She wanted Bradley to think she was calm and rational and going with the program.

"The FBI wants this man, and Jack can identify him."

And now I can too. She kept the thought to herself. "Is the FBI here?" she asked. The FBI had to be helpful. Someone was stalking Jack in a mall full of people, ordinary people, happy people, her friends, and his, little kids: people who could get hurt.

"Yes," he said. Then he swore again. She strained to listen to the conversation. Apparently, Jack's black box wasn't moving, and Jack wasn't responding. The man reporting to Bradley couldn't see Jack or the box.

"What was the man wearing?" he asked her.

She told him, and he relayed the details to the others.

"Shouldn't you be out there?" she asked. "What about Soldier? Why is Soldier with that other man?"

Bradley ignored her, but he let go of her arm. Mari slipped her phone out of her pocket. She had a team too. She texted Omar.

A little help. Gift wrapping table.

Bradley peered around the edge of the curtain at the entrance to their hiding spot. She was right. He wanted to be out there. If he didn't have to guard her, he would be. That would be good for Jack. Jack needed help. She remembered how Jack's team had hustled him out of the supermarket the day they met.

She crouched down behind Bradley, looking out through the slit he'd created between the curtain and the wall. What she saw was the box of Santa hats under the gift-wrapping table. And then Omar arrived in one of the mall's electric utility carts.

He hopped down, pulled the box of Santa hats from under the table, and lifted the curtain into their space, ready to push the box inside. He came face-to-face with Bradley. Omar's gaze shifted to Mari.

"I'm okay," she said, "but there's a situation. We need help. This is Bradley. He's a security guy. Bradley, Omar, head of mall facilities." The two men did a staring thing. Apparently, Omar's mall shirt and badge satisfied Bradley.

"What's the help you need, Ms. Lynch?" Omar asked.

"We need to find a small black box that's somewhere between A-12 and A-10," she told him.

Bradley nodded.

"No walkie-talkies. Text only." Mari held up her phone, warning Omar.

Omar took off in the cart. Bradley kept up a low conversation with his team. Mari tried to think of ways to help Jack. Maybe the electric carts. Maybe Mari could call store managers, get them to close up early, tell them something, get people moving for the exits without a panic. Maybe a computer glitch.

She was thinking about issuing a "Lost Parent" announcement when Omar pulled up in the cart. He came through the curtain, one latex-gloved hand extended holding the black box. Bradley reached for it, but Omar held on.

"Careful." He set the box down on top of the box of Santa hats. "There's blood on it."

Mari stared at the little box. Jack was hurt, bleeding, and unable to send messages. They had to get to him.

Bradley pressed Omar for details about where he'd found the box and relayed the information to his network. As he talked with the others, Mari slid along the wall. She'd almost reached the opening when Bradley swung his gaze back to her.

"Stay here, miss," he ordered in that voice of male command that always expected obedience. "We think Ryker managed to get away from his assailant. We're sending Soldier to look for him." He stepped through the curtain.

Soldier was a good move, but Jack was still out there, still alone, still wounded, still being hunted by a bad guy, and Mari had no intention of staying where Bradley put her. She just needed a way to get past Bradley. If she could slip behind him into the crowd, she would still need a way to get out into the mall.

She stared at the Santa hat box with its bloody burden until a crazy idea came to her. After stuffing Jack's small black box in her slacks pocket, she opened the big hat box, grabbed a Santa hat, and tucked it under her T-shirt. On the other side of the curtain, Bradley stood with his back to her, looking down the mall. His voice made a low rumble as he talked to his crew, and he gave no sign that he had detected her handling of the box.

She slipped out of the alcove, squeezing into the crowd, working her way toward the singers. As they finished their set, the crowd burst into applause, and the boys took their bows. Mari positioned herself, waiting. When they started a new song, the crowd parted to let the boys through, and Mari pulled out the Santa hat, put it on, and strolled away down the main mall aisle with the C-Notes.

Chapter 18

Jack grabbed a handful of paper napkins from the cider cart and threaded his way deeper into the cookware store. He turned his back to a wall of copper pots and stuffed the wad of napkins up under his sweater, between the wound in his side and his belt. He was lucky. The lost black box had skewed Evans's angle with the knife. Evans would be angry, and his next move would be to change his appearance. That was how he operated. Somewhere he would have stashed a change of clothes. And he'd likely change his hair or add some glasses.

The new Evans, furious and improvising, the one Mari would not recognize, would come for her. Jack didn't know from which end of the mall Evans would approach. He'd lost sight of the man when the cider lady's intervention separated them. He'd lost his Santa hat as well. Jack's gut clenched. A powerful wave of dizziness blurred his vision, and he gripped the edge of the wooden table in front of him.

The weakness passed. He relaxed his grip and positioned himself behind a towering display of boxed gingerbread house kits. From there he could see the entrance and people passing in the main walkway. He couldn't see the bin where Evans had tossed the black box. His guys would zero in on that, tempted to move to it, and when they did, Evans would be waiting and watching for a chance to go after Mari. Jack had to be ready to stop him.

***

Halfway down the mall, Mari stepped away from the C-Notes. Only one boy, the one with the dark-tinted shades, glanced back at her, his face puzzled. The rest sauntered on toward the south end of the mall. Mari gave the boy a quick wave. She had a new idea now. It had come to her as the boys sang. She didn't know exactly how it worked, but the black box in her slacks' pocket meant that Jack's team would track her position. The box's movement might puzzle them, but they would follow it. With the Santa hat and her black T-shirt, she would become the target, a pseudo-Jack. She kept her head lowered, counting on the Santa hat to catch the eye of Jack's enemy. It was a crazy plan, but it might work. If the wavy-haired man followed her instead of Jack, she and the black box would lead him straight into the arms of Jack's team. At least that was her new plan.

Mari kept her gaze on the place where she'd last seen Jack, moving as slowly as she imagined Jack would, trying not to tense up when she sensed movement behind her. She was sure the mall sound system had become stuck on the line about silver bells from the chorus of "It's Christmas time in the city." She felt lifted out of the stream of time, stuck in the moment, incapable of moving past fear and tension. Men and women rushed by, burdened with multiple shopping bags, checking their phones, intent perhaps on finding some last-minute item before heading home to dinner. If the man after Jack was out there, he had the perfect cover. No one paid attention to anyone else.

When she came abreast of the stand of artificial trees in the center of the walkway, a hand seized her shoulder in a brutal grip. A man's voice spoke in her ear. "Thank you, Ms. Lynch, you've saved me some trouble."

She froze, her pulse racing, her stomach cramping, her knees shaky. She recognized the voice instantly: the wavy-haired man with the walkie-talkie at his waist.

"Smile. Keep walking," he said. "We're going to find Ryker."

She kept her gaze forward, searching for anyone she knew, anyone on Jack's team. Bradley and the others should be looking for the box by now. Ahead, one of Omar's white electric carts moved slowly toward Santa's workshop. She couldn't see the driver or any mall security guards. She looked for Jack's friends in the line of Santa visitors, now much shorter, but didn't see them. There was no sign of the dark-skinned man with Soldier. Maybe she was wrong about the box in her pocket. Maybe it didn't work automatically as she'd imagined. She brushed her hand against it.

Her assailant jerked her to a halt outside the cookware shop. He seemed to consider his next move. Mari stared at the floor. A smattering of dark red drops made a trail past the open doors into the store. She didn't know whether he noticed. He had ditched his walkie-talkie or turned it off because she no longer heard its crackle. Then his voice at her ear said, "Inside. Smile. Touch nothing, and no one gets hurt."

He pushed her through the open doors. He was lying about not hurting anyone. He'd already hurt Jack, and he would do worse, but maybe she could keep him from hurting the people around them. Doreen, the greeter in her green apron, had her back to them, putting away her cider cart. The high-ceilinged store was sizeable, but not the largest in the mall. Towering stacks of products on wooden islands might give Jack some cover, but not for long. Past the entrance, the trail of blood disappeared.

Shoppers holding stacks of items to be purchased lined up around the main counter while clerks worked rapidly to ring up sales, everyone intent on those transactions, everyone oblivious. No one glanced at Mari and the man pushing her forward. That had to be good. If the bad guy didn't feel noticed or threatened, he wouldn't lash out at anyone else. She kept her smile in place.

Her captor used his grip on her shoulder to steer her to the left around the sales counter, and Mari searched the displays for anything she could grab and use against him. She glanced at the knives in their locked glass display cabinet, tantalizingly out of reach. They passed tall stacks of Santa mugs and containers of red and green spatulas. Her captor seemed to know where he was going, but they were running out of store. To her left was a head-high tower of red and white tins of toffees and caramel-coated popcorn. A few yards in front of her was the entry to the stockroom. From it, an exit led to a loading area and the dark employee parking lot. She had no intention of ending up alone in the parking lot with her captor.

Opposite the candy tins to her right, a final product display counter crammed with botanical hand soaps and lotions in seasonal scents offered her one last chance. Mari reached for an open tester bottle.

Simultaneously, the head-high stack of candy tins at her left elbow collapsed. Her ears rang with the clatter, and a heavy can bounced off her foot and rolled away. Her captor grunted, the grip on her shoulder loosened, and she stumbled forward, grabbed the nearest soap tester bottle, and spun to face him—and stopped.

With his back to her, Jack stood between her and the man. For a confused moment, looking over Jack's shoulder, Mari didn't recognize the other man. His clothes and his light brown hair slicked straight back from his forehead didn't match her memory.

"Ryker," he said. The voice was the same. He smiled, and Mari recognized the gleam of lethal intent in his eyes. It *was* the same man. He held a narrow dark blade nearly concealed against gray slacks.

In the next instant, he grabbed Jack's collar and yanked. Jack shot out a hand to counter the knife as the man lunged, and their bodies smacked together. Mari flung her arm over Jack's shoulder, shoved the plastic soap container in the man's face, and pumped. Anger spurted out of her, scented like lavender and cedarwood. The man twisted his head and loosed his grip on Jack, trying to bat her arm away. She didn't stop. His face disappeared under jets of pale creamy soap, and he staggered back and dropped to his knees, writhing, clinging to the knife with one hand and reaching with his other to pull his shirt up to his face.

Jack dipped under Mari's arm, and his weight shifted as they both tilted dangerously, then his back stiffened and held, as if he'd found control over gravity itself. He straightened and kicked the man's knife hand, sending the blade sliding across the floor into the fallen candy tins.

From the back of the store, Soldier bounded past Mari and Jack, pouncing on the fallen man, seizing his jacket in his teeth, and yanking him backward to the floor. At Jack's command, Soldier released the man and stood over him, teeth still bared, panting.

Jack lifted Mari's arm from his shoulder and turned her around.

She pressed her face to his chest and let him hold her, his arms tight. It was over. He was safe. He was whole. Against her ear she felt the pounding of his heart and her own. She wanted to let go of the soap dispenser, but her hand had cramped around it.

In the next moment, Jack's team surrounded them, along with three men in suits Mari had never seen before. The men made a human wall around them, behind which voices rose in a confused babble. Walkie-talkies squawked. The strangers took charge. One, wearing latex gloves, collected the knife in a plastic bag. Another summoned the paramedics, placed the fallen man in handcuffs, and hauled him to his feet. An EMT shouldered his way into the circle, wiped the fallen man's face, and began to rinse his eyes. The third stranger issued orders on his phone.

Everything seemed to happen at a great distance, far from the little island of safety she and Jack inhabited. His heartbeat grew steady. Her fingers released their grip on the soap dispenser, and she dropped it.

Omar appeared. She heard him speak calmly to the store manager as the babble subsided.

Then Bradley spoke in his usual terse manner. "Let's get you out of here, Ryker, miss." Mari lifted her head from Jack's chest. "The FBI wants a statement from you, Ms. Lynch. The paramedics will see to your wound, Ryker."

"Right," Jack said.

Then Bradley, cinder block Bradley, broke into a grin. "We got him," he said. "Evans is in custody." He held out his hand, and Jack shook it. Then he turned to Mari.

"Soap, huh? Not mace, exactly, but it worked."

Chapter 19

Jack's team and one of the strangers, who turned out to be an Agent Arias from the FBI, hustled Mari and Jack out of the store's rear entrance to an electric cart. Omar drove them to the employee community room where an ambulance and a firetruck, their lights flashing, stood parked outside.

Inside, Agent Arias settled Mari at one of the familiar round tables that dotted the room. He saw that she got a cup of coffee and coaxed her to give her statement while paramedics worked on Jack. She explained the black box and turned it over to Arias. People came and went around them, speaking in low, earnest voices. Her boss showed up to express relief and concern. Answering Arias, unable to touch Jack, she lost track of the time. Images flashed in her mind—the malice in Evans's eyes, the knife in his hand, the moment he lunged for Jack.

Across the community room, the paramedics stripped Jack of his sweater, a protective black vest around his torso, and his bloodstained T-shirt. They asked questions, took his vitals, hooked him up to an IV drip, and examined his wound. His gaze never left Mari. Within a few minutes, he was bandaged and seated facing her across the distance that separated them while the IV solution went into his arm. A paramedic draped a dark blue blanket over Jack's shoulders, and one of his team brought him a cup of something to drink. Somewhere along the way, she and Jack had lost their Santa hats.

Bradley leaned down and whispered in Jack's ear. Jack gave a thumbs-up, and the dark-skinned man appeared with Soldier. The dog settled between Jack's legs and nudged Jack's hand until he stroked the dog's ears. The man said something to make Jack grin and laugh, and then wince. Jack's friends, Huntington and Sloan, appeared at the entrance to the community room with the two women Mari had met earlier, and the blond-headed kid.

"Excuse me, Ms. Lynch," Agent Arias said. "Let me move the gawkers away."

"No," she said. "They're okay. They're Jack's family." They were. He didn't belong to her in spite of the danger they had shared. His friends, his team, even Soldier had a prior claim on Jack.

Arias frowned as if he'd insist on keeping an official barrier around Jack, but Bradley intervened, bringing Huntington and Sloan across the room. They made a striking pair, one ruggedly, darkly handsome, the other all golden good looks. The men talked with all the ease of familiarity, of knowing one another well. Soldier trotted from Jack over to the little boy, who knelt to hug him. It was Mari who was outside the circle of closeness around Jack. She turned back to Arias.

But she couldn't concentrate. Jack's friends left, and the dog came back to him. The IV dripped into Jack's arm. She wanted to be alone with him, but they were going nowhere until the bag of solution was empty. At last Arias finished getting her statement. He handed her his card, telling her that he would be in touch. When she asked if Evans would be blind, if his eyes would be okay, Arias frowned and told her not to worry about Frank Evans. The man would get any treatment he needed in custody.

The ringing of her phone in her pocket startled her. She'd forgotten the outside world existed. It was her dad wanting to know if she was okay. Her parents had heard from Shanny that there had been a serious incident at the mall, and Mari felt sudden tears burn. Her strained conversation with her dad over her grandpa had been her last talk with anyone in her family, and she hadn't thought to call them. She'd been focused entirely on Jack. She reassured her dad and looked up from her phone to find Jack's puzzled gaze on her. She wiped her eyes. The community room seemed huge, and Jack, impossibly distant on the other side of it. She loved him, but loving him was not like any other experience of love she'd had. She was used to the kind of love made up of small acts and attentions: her mother brushing her hair, her dad reading her a story, her grandpa teaching her to bait a hook. She was used to love in the shore break, her feet on the ground, gentle waves around her ankles. For Jack, if she wanted him, she was going to have to plunge in and let the waves take her, sometimes knocking her heart about, and sometimes lifting it and sending it scudding light as air, light as foam. She got to her feet and headed for Jack.

"What is it?" He took her hand in his.

"My family," she said, relieved to be touching him. "I forgot about them."

"Do you need to go home?" he asked. "The guys can take you."

"No." She let her gaze say that she needed to be with him.

"We'll go to your place then."

She nodded. More people came and went around them. Jack told Bradley their plan, and asked him to get a car ready. Her phone pinged. Absently, she checked the sender and slid the phone back into her pocket.

When the paramedics returned to unhook Jack from the IV, Mari roused herself to ask about caring for the wound, giving pain meds, and getting Jack seen by a doctor. Bradley showed up to say that the SUV would take them to her place. Mari retrieved her purse and coat from her office, and Jack's team led them away. No one took her phone.

***

In the rain-soaked alley behind Mari's place, Jack's team dropped them off. Mari, keys in hand, went ahead down the path to her door as Jack stood wrapped in the paramedics' blanket and his bloodstained khakis, rubbing Soldier's ears in parting. He needed a few things and asked Bradley to bring them. His guys were ready to celebrate and to mourn. He knew they felt the elation of victory over Evans, but they felt sorrow, too, for the friends who were not there to see it, who were never coming back. The end of the mission and the fellowship was a bittersweet mix. Tomorrow or the next day he would find a way to say good-bye to the team they had been. Tonight, he needed Mari. As the SUV pulled away, he turned back to her.

He found her leaning her head against the apartment door, trying with a shaking hand to fit her key in the lock, and she glanced over her shoulder at him. "I don't know why my legs are so shaky. It's over, isn't it?"

"It's the…aftermath." He put his hand on hers and turned the key. The lock clicked, and he pushed the door open. The smell of

Christmas tree rushed over them, fresh and woodsy, a breath of forest, an antidote to evil.

She asked if he could handle the stairs alone.

"You go ahead," he said. "I'll make it."

She kicked off her shoes and went up ahead of him. He watched the sway of her hips until she passed out of his sight. A light went on at the top of the stairs, and he heard her moving around. Now that they were alone, he sensed some uncertainty in her about how things stood between them. Her shakes probably came as much from thinking about what lay ahead as from what had passed. He hoisted himself up the stairs and waited for her in her living room, in front of the Christmas tree, bare except for the Santa ornament he'd given her. He took that Santa as a good sign. In a few minutes, she came back, and her gaze went straight to his.

"You kept it," he said.

She nodded. "Can I get you something to eat? A sandwich, an omelet? I don't know…something?"

"No." He couldn't think about food yet. He considered her loveseat, and her gaze followed his. "It's small."

"It's a small apartment."

"It's not a 'sofa.'" He watched as his meaning registered, and her cheeks flushed.

"Oh, oh, I see what you mean. I do have a bed."

It was time to put everything he wanted to the test. He needed to keep her with him always. Before Evans went after her, Jack had thought he could let her go and return to his former life, but that guarded half-life was gone. He held out a hand. She took it, and he pulled her close, looking for a sign in her eyes. "Do you think you could marry a man like me?"

"Like you? How like you?"

He tried to read the expression in her eyes. His breath grew tight in his chest, and he made himself name the things he was. "Awkward. Damaged. Undeserving. Wrong for you."

"Wrong for me?"

"Your family will think so. They won't approve."

She didn't deny it. "My mom is going to see the tattoos." She traced them with her fingertips. He swallowed hard. His greedy imagination wanted that touch everywhere.

"And she'll ask—*Does this boy have a college degree?* My dad will see the hair and wonder whether we've slept together." She laid her open hand over his heart, and smiled up at him. "I don't know any men 'like' you. But I know you. It's crazy, but I do, and yes, I could marry you." Her gaze was solemn, but her smile widened. "Of course, you'd have to propose."

He was silent. First, he had to tell her the whole truth about himself. "There are things I have to tell you."

"Okay." Her eyes hid nothing: she was wary of his further revelations. He didn't deserve her love. He just wanted it, like a gift from the universe, from some Santa Claus for grown-up boys who'd not asked for anything in a long time.

He pulled her to the loveseat, then draped the blanket he'd been wearing over one of the loveseat's tall square arms and arranged them the way he liked: his back against the arm, his legs stretched out, nestling Mari between them with her back to him. The knife wound smarted, but he could handle it. Almost at once, she began to shake, and he wrapped his arms around her and held on.

"It's the adrenaline," he said.

"I was so angry, so afraid." She shuddered. "I see his eyes. I see the knife."

"Why did you come after him? I sent Bradley to keep you safe."

"I came after *you*, not him. I saw you standing there alone even before Evans came up to you. You should have been with everyone else, with your friends, with me. I thought, not consciously, but still…I thought, you needed a team, like the characters in your game. When Evans grabbed your shoulder, I didn't understand why you let him take you. But I knew he was the reason you kept yourself to yourself—alone."

"I had to let him take me." He spoke gently. "The fault was mine. I had to take the blame. I'm the one who let him loose in this world, your world. For years he operated abroad, doing deals in Tashkent and Abu Dhabi. I took that away. So he came after me, and then he went after those who helped me."

"They rescued you? Bradley and the others?"

"Yes, from…that hut. Two of their friends died."

"I wanted to hurt him. I couldn't stop squirting the soap, I hated him so. I hated that he could bring danger to people I love, that he could take you away from me."

"I was supposed to stop him before he could hurt anyone else. Instead, I led him to you. I don't know if you can forgive me."

She shifted in his arms, taking his hands in hers. "I have."

For a suspended moment he simply breathed her in. Her answer contained the thing he'd seen in her from the beginning, the thing he'd wanted before he'd understood what it was. She didn't need a perfect man, a perfect family, a perfect grandfather. Her way of loving began with acceptance.

"I want to make love to you," he said. "You know that."

"I rather hoped you felt that way."

"The thing is…" He plunged ahead. "I haven't done it before."

"Made love to me?" Her voice was puzzled.

"Made love."

She went very still in his arms, taking it in, getting his full meaning. He could sense her brain working furiously, reviewing their times together.

"I'm pretty sure I can manage the basics. I might not be…I don't know…cool, smooth."

She twisted around in his hold, coming to her knees, facing him. A twinge of pain shot up his side. "You," she said. "You could have died today. Without ever…without ever…being loved by me, the way I want to love you."

A sob shook her, and she pounded his chest with her fists, each blow echoing through his body, jarring his wounds, until he caught her hands and pulled her mouth down to his.

***

Jack kissed her until she melted against him. He wasn't dead. He was alive and aching for her. She gave a final hiccup of a sob and lay still in his arms. He stroked her back. Her cheek lay against his bare chest, and her hair was silky under his jaw. Her angry fists had opened until her fingers curled loosely, softly, over the swell of his bicep. Her breathing grew steady.

Peace, he thought. They were experiencing peace after a storm. There were no cameras and no guards. He had no black box on his hip, no dog at his side, no chair to hold him in rigid balance, nothing to remind him of the tension under which he had lived for nearly four years. The dark Christmas tree with its battered Santa stood as a lone sentry over them.

After a time, she stirred. “Are you going to explain how you skipped over the having sex chapter of growing up?” she asked.

“Later.”

“Am I hurting you?”

He wasn’t hurting. Her hip rested against his arousal. “I don’t want to bleed on your loveseat,” he said.

She gave a tiny laugh and righted herself in his hold. The movement sent a dizzying jolt of pleasure through him, and he sucked in a breath and closed his eyes, holding the pleasure in, prolonging the moment.

She rested a hand on his chest. “Should we move to the bed?”

He swallowed and let out a raspy syllable of agreement.

“I want to shower first.” She stood. “Is that crazy? I want Evans’s touch gone.”

“Not crazy. I can wait. Bradley’s bringing me some…things.”

“Okay. You can eat…or…whatever…”

“Go.”

She hesitated a second. “You will explain later.” She disappeared around the corner of the living room.

He steadied himself and swung his legs to the floor, looking around, getting a sense of the layout of her apartment. The entry stairs divided the apartment in half. In front of him was an opening into a dining area separated from the living room by a half wall in front of which stood the tree with his Santa. To his right a sliding glass door opened onto a deck over the alley.

From somewhere to his left in the parts of the apartment he hadn’t yet seen, a shower began running. His mind flashed on Mari standing naked under a stream of warm water, flashed on joining her, on the slide of slick, soapy skin against skin. He readied himself to stand, and the wound in his back let him know that a shower with her would have to wait. A knock sounded at her door, and he went to answer it.

A canvas bag sat on the doormat. Bradley had delivered. Jack collected it and headed back up the stairs toward her bedroom. As he entered, the whine of a hair dryer came from behind a closed pocket door on his right. Her coat lay over the arm of a padded wicker chair, and for a moment he simply stood, touching her coat because he could, arrested by thoughts of her. A glass lamp on a table next to the quilt-covered bed lit a feminine retreat, a softened world, far different from his stark fortress. She had a long low bookshelf under her window, crammed with books, its top lined with shells and driftwood and framed photos. He would have to make some changes to his world if he wanted her to share his fortress with him.

The pocket door that led to the bathroom slid open, and she came out, wrapped in a large white towel and a swirl of peppermint-scented steam. She caught and held his gaze. "Did you get the things you needed?"

"I did." He put the bag from Bradley on the chair. He'd already checked the bag's contents.

"I've been thinking," she said.

"Tell me," he invited.

"Maybe you've already figured out…how you…want to do this."

"I've given it some thought," he admitted. He couldn't help a brief grin. That was part of her effect on him. For a long time, he'd made himself unfamiliar with the giving and receiving of smiles. Now his mouth naturally quirked upward in her presence.

"I mean because of your…balance issues. You never turn your head…and your back is hurting. Before, we stood against the wall."

He'd thought of all the things she mentioned, his limitations, the difficulties, and still he wanted her under him in bed. He was pretty sure he'd figured out how to do it. Not taking his gaze from hers, he undid the fastenings on his khakis, let them drop to the floor, and carefully disentangled his feet.

Her gaze skimmed his body—his scarred torso, the bandage around his waist, the place where his erection tented his boxers, his bloodied knee—and came back to meet his. He recognized that gaze for what it was: an act of love. Because she loved him, whether she said it or not, he could offer her his damaged earthbound body, his imperfect self.

"Come here," he said.

The air stirred as she came to him, bringing her scent and warmth, and he stepped forward to meet her. He brought her body up against his. She tilted her face to his, and her mouth opened to him, welcoming. He kissed her until he grew shaky with the need for more.

"Let me touch you?" he asked. Once they reached the bed, he would be limited again. She nodded, and he turned her in his arms and held her against him, pulling the towel away. He cupped her breasts and ran his thumbs over the peaks, then he stroked down over her belly. In reply, she sighed and reached between them, brushing a hand over his erection. His whole body shook in reaction. Vague knowledge coalesced into certainty, and he slid his fingers down into the curls at the warm, moist juncture of her thighs, finding a way to please her.

She sucked in a breath and twisted back to face him, taking his hands and drawing him to the bed. While she tossed aside the pillows and drew back the covers, he retrieved the condoms from the bag on the chair. He shed his boxers and sat on the edge of the bed, his hands unsteady as he tore the package on a condom until she wrapped her hands around his and took over the intimate task. Sheathed and breathless, he waited for the mattress to dip under her weight, for the final invitation to join her. It came, not with words, but with the gentle touch of her palm against his spine above his bandaged waist.

There was an awkward moment as he positioned himself beside her. He couldn't speak, but he knew what to do. Pushing up from the bed on arms made strong from endless training, he made his body a canopy, a shelter under which she could lie. *This* he wanted to say, *this is what I will be to you.*

She understood, and in a heartbeat, slid under him, and it was his turn to look and hers to touch. Beneath him, she was dusky hollows and creamy curves, and a pulse beating at the base of her throat. A warm glow lit her eyes, and her lips parted in a small, knowing smile. He held himself above her while she stroked up and down his chest, then cupped his sex in her palms, running her thumbs along his length. At the touch, his body flexed, and he gritted his teeth to keep from passing out from pleasure.

Shaking, he lowered his hips to meet hers, letting her guide their joining. Her body closed around his with complete and trusting acceptance. Then he could hold back no longer. He rocked into her, and her breathing changed, punctuated by little catches and soft cries. Her body arched and tightened, and her hands came around him, sliding down to hold his hips. He held himself back in spite of the tremors shaking him, waiting for her, judging her need by his own. Her face grew fierce with concentration, and still he waited, hovering on the brink of being forever changed. Words he'd never thought to say sprang to his lips.

"I love you," he said.

Her body shuddered around his in reply, and he let go. His release rocketed him past gravity's reach, so that he floated, weightless, buoyant, tethered only by the love in her eyes. For a timeless moment he knew nothing of his faults and weaknesses, only that he was loved.

Chapter 20

With a bit of fumbling and laughter, they left the rumpled bed, managing the mundane details of reentry to emerge changed. At least, Mari knew she'd changed. She loved him. It was that simple. Her friends might say she was merely feeling the afterglow of really good sex, but she didn't think so. She loved him for the way he was openly vulnerable with her, the way ordinary joys surprised him, the way he touched Soldier's ears, the way he kissed her as if each kiss were a small miracle. It even seemed right that her virgin lover had left a spot of blood on her sheets from his injured knee.

He pulled a T-shirt and unstained khakis from the bag his friend brought, and she put on a sleep shirt over flannel PJ bottoms. They returned to the loveseat, still descending from the high, and nested in the way he preferred: her back against his chest, his arms around her. It wasn't skin to skin, but that closeness could wait until he explained how he'd come to share this first with her. "You just skipped the sex part of growing up? A whole chapter?"

"I read the CliffsNotes."

She felt his smile though she couldn't see it. "Lucky for you you've got that bandage around your middle. Otherwise, I would have to jab you in the ribs for that comment."

"There were no girls at Canyon. The only available sex was in books. We had these old, blue, hardbound dictionaries. You got your dictionary in ninth grade and put your name inside the cover. In study hall, we sat in rows on hard chairs with our dictionaries out, looking at the clock and finding all the words with sexual content. Illustrations were encouraged. I learned a lot."

Mari could tell from the change in his voice that the past had claimed him for the moment. "So, sex was…a joke?"

"To my classmates. I was small at thirteen. I got pounded a lot. So mostly, I kept my mouth shut. I did find one word everyone else missed."

"What?"

"*Priapism*. Basically, that's Greek for a four-hour erection."

She laughed. "There really were no girls? No 'sister' schools? No female teachers, secretaries?"

"There were a few female employees at school. You met Sloan's wife, Annie: she worked in admissions. I didn't like the way men treated those women. I didn't want to be that kind of man." He slid his hand up and down her arm, fingertips brushing the side of her breast. He'd been speaking naturally without pauses. Now he lapsed back to the irregular pattern of their first conversations, his speech broken by unexpected gaps. She held her breath.

"My father was one of those men, and Headmaster Chambers. They hurt my mom. She starred in a few of my father's black comedy thrillers before I was born, but he betrayed her. And…" At the mention of his mother, he tensed and fell silent. Mari waited, finding his hand and taking it in hers.

"Before junior year, my mom gave a pool party for my class, and after that, the guys liked to joke about who wanted to sleep with her. I… Two nights before graduation…I burned down the school sign."

"Ah," she said, keeping her voice light in spite of the ache in her throat for the boy whose adolescence had apparently been a sustained cocktail of anger, helplessness, and profound loneliness. "What you needed was a pair of mother fangs."

"Is that what you have? Did I miss something here?"

"I'm not a mother. I hope to be someday, but even little girls start growing the fangs. They're retractable. No one sees them under the frills on our dresses and the sparkles on our shoes, and when we start wearing makeup and sweaters, they really don't notice, but mess with someone we love, and the fangs come out."

His hand stopped moving on her arm, then started again. "With someone you love, huh."

"Yes." She might as well admit it. "Evans never stood a chance."

"So you didn't need those mother fangs before now?"

"Maybe to defend my grandpa."

"Not to defend your ex?"

Oh, she knew he would get to that. She wanted more of Jack's story. He hadn't explained the ten years after high school, but to be fair, she needed to return the favor and tell him something about her past. What could she say? She hadn't lived in a fancy house or gone to a snooty school, and yet her childhood had been a picnic compared to his, with nothing to vex or trouble her except ordinary woes and losses. Her grandparents' divorce had been the worst of it. Her parents loved each other and their children. She hadn't known until she met Jack how her grandpa had hurt her family.

Jack had admitted things to her, shocking things, soul-damaging things. She could hardly offer up the same level of revelations out of her sheltered existence. Her sins were shallow and ordinary, and she fervently hoped not so hurtful that anyone ended up damaged or dead. But maybe that could be her gift to him, a confession of those daily faults, tiny acts of selfishness that caused others discomfort or unhappiness.

"There were boyfriends, you know, and dark corners here and there. In high school, I was mostly good at crushes, unrequited love, at picking someone above my pay grade and loving from afar. Eye contact was a big deal."

"And later?"

"Things were different. Are you sure you want to hear this?"

"I need to know."

"For a long time, everything was very temporary, very in the moment, and always…disappointing. So, when Grant, my ex, suggested we get an apartment together, it seemed like commitment, like being a grown-up. And when we found a place, I thought we were making a life together. I don't think guys make that mistake: the mistake of thinking that because you're sharing appliances and utility bills, you're actually in a relationship. Anyway, he found us a fabulous sofa…"

Jack's hand stopped moving.

Mari laughed. "We never had sex on that sofa, so you don't have to feel—"

"Like I have to knock him down?"

"The thing is, the sofa wasn't really ours. He'd borrowed it from a real estate stager. And one day it went away, and if I'd been paying attention, I would have realized that I was sort of like that sofa in his life, useful on a temporary basis, a starter wife, not a permanent part of his plan. That was a year ago, right after Christmas."

He was silent. She had no idea what he was thinking, how foolish and careless she appeared. She'd been playing at love. She hadn't really known Grant, and he'd actually made no promises to her. To him their time together had been a living arrangement. She'd been a convenience that had allowed him to concentrate on his MBA program. He wasn't responsible for her wrong assumptions.

"Maybe I don't have to knock him down," Jack said. "Maybe I should thank him. He kept you tied up until I came along."

"Are you turning forgiving on me? No more burning down signs and tracking down enemies?"

"I'm a changed man. As long as no one tries to hurt you."

***

Midday Monday morning, Mari sat in her office, hunched over her computer, dealing with a tsunami of email complaints from merchants, staff, and customers. Her boss had sent her a big floral arrangement with a card of congratulations for her part in nabbing Evans, but he'd also left a voicemail message reminding her that two shopping days remained.

Her door opened and Rachel and Shanny walked in.

"We're taking you for coffee. Our treat," Shanny said. She reached for Mari's bag, and Mari offered only a feeble protest. She was happy to let her friends drag her off to the bistro. The three had been retail warriors together through three Christmas seasons, and when they had their lattes and the usual basket of the bistro's signature oversize muffins in front of them, her friends grew serious.

"We want to be sure that you're okay." Rachel spread cream cheese on an orange zest muffin.

"We don't want you making another big boyfriend mistake." Shanny broke a banana-chocolate chip into steaming halves. "So, tell us everything."

"Start with what actually happened on Saturday," Rachel said. "The police log says that officers were called to a 'disturbance' at the mall. Sounds like a cover-up to me."

"What everyone's saying," Shanny added, "was that a guy came after you with a knife and you blasted him in the eyes with hand soap."

Mari nodded. That much of the story had probably circulated among the staff and merchants. She'd been warned by Agent Arias not to say too much, but she needed to reassure her friends. She took a deep breath and began to tell them what she could. What mattered wasn't what happened with the knife and the hand soap and Evans or the FBI, though those things made the story dramatic; what mattered was she and Jack had been changed by what happened.

"So, then what? You just fell into each other's arms?" Shanny's question sounded like an accusation.

Mari nodded. She put it as simply as she could. "Jack stepped between me and this man. He put his body between a knife and me."

"So, the sex is that good?" Shanny wanted to know.

Mari lifted her coffee cup to hide a smile. It was good.

"Shanny," Rachel protested.

"Well, it must be," Shanny insisted. "We, your friends, were worried sick, and you went all radio silence on us for twenty-four hours."

It was true. Mari could see it in their faces. She hadn't meant to forget them exactly, her friends or her family. The new feelings for Jack had simply consumed her in a way she'd never been consumed before. "I'm sorry. It wasn't all sex. We did a lot of talking."

"It all seems so risky and not at all like you, Mari." Rachel frowned.

"Oh Mari, you're not going to move in with him, are you?" Shanny asked. "You've made that mistake before."

"We can't give you up to just anyone," Rachel said.

"He's not just… Wait, I have a picture of him that his friend sent me." She reached into her bag and pulled out her phone. "You'll see. Jack is not at all like Grant."

"Still, you knew Grant. You hardly know this Jack," Rachel suggested in her gentle way.

"Isn't he basically a weirdo?" Shanny's voice was plaintive. "A hot weirdo, but still a weirdo."

Mari handed her phone to Rachel, and her friends bent their heads over it. They fell silent, looking at the image of Jack holding the puppy. Mari waited. She was counting on the picture to show Jack's true nature. If she couldn't convince her friends, how would she convince her family?

"Well, apparently dogs like him. That's something," Shanny admitted. "You know your parents are going to see the hair and the tats."

"I know. Jack may not look like the kind of man who's right for me, but he's the one." She knew it was true. Her head was unexpectedly clear.

Rachel handed back Mari's phone. "We'll meet him, right?"

"Before you do anything stupid," Shanny added.

"Very soon." Mari tucked her phone away. She had to be patient with her friends. She had to have faith that people she loved, who loved her, could learn to love Jack.

***

From his window above the Strand, Jack watched the sea stretch gray and glossy to the horizon under a slight overcast sky. Each smooth new wave broke as a distinct episode in the ocean's long history. Lovemaking, he mused, might be as ordinary and fleeting as those waves. It was something human beings had always done, but he thought he'd remember each time with Mari the way surfers remembered individual waves.

He had hours yet before he'd see her again.

In the morning, he'd surprised his guys by walking back from her apartment along the Strand without Soldier, without a cane or sticks, and without a black box on his hip. It hadn't been a perfect performance. He'd had to stop more than once, but he'd done it without falling down. The guys had expected him to call for a ride. When the house cameras picked him up, Bradley had rushed out to meet him, and then they both had grinned. Evans was locked up. Jack was free.

He was free to start a new life. By noon he had a new phone and a thousand things to do. He texted Mari at once that he wanted to meet her family. He wanted her to meet his unexpected second family, Sloan and Huntington and the women they loved, and Mae, Sloan's mom, and Max, the kid Huntington was going to adopt. He didn't want to spend another night of his life apart from her, but he'd heard her history, so he couldn't be sure she was as ready as he was to make that move. Still, he put things in motion to tip the scales in favor of having her with him on the Strand.

In between calls, he talked with each of the team about what came next. Marcus and Miguel were going to stay on as a skeleton staff. Cole worked locally with other clients and would remain available for Jack's training and continuing rehab. Bradley had caught the attention of the mall's management, and they'd invited him to do some security consulting for Coast Plaza. Rashaad would continue to run the day-to-day operations of their video-game development company. The field was booming. There was new interest in games for training as well as recovery, and in areas like surgery and policing, and a whole movement of game developers who were pushing to make games fully accessible to players with all sorts of differences, not just psychological damage.

The guys were ready to move on, too, but first they had a tradition they wanted to observe, modified, of course, because he wasn't a marine and they were, to the core and forever. His presence was requested at a special meal for which he was to dress formally. No flip-flops. Oh, and he could expect merciless ribbing. He probably deserved it, certainly deserved it. And he welcomed the dinner. It would help him pass the remaining hours until Mari was released from her job.

Now, good smells came from the kitchen, causing Soldier's nose to twitch. The table where he and Mari had had their first date had been extended to accommodate the whole team and set with linens, plates, and silverware from Jack's parents' house. He took another look at the ocean and glanced at a new message on his phone. *See you soon* she'd texted.

Behind him the door opened, and the festivities began. Marcus was the "President" of the event, and Nick was the "Vice." They gave him a cranberry juice punch so that he could participate in the toasts—to the President of the United States, to the colonel, to their lost comrades, and to the other branches of the services. There was a toast to Soldier, and a toast to the confusion of the enemy. The solemnity of the toasts declined a bit as glasses were raised repeatedly.

Then Rashaad rose to his feet. "Sir, permission to address the mess."

"Granted," said Marcus in his role as President.

"In 2012 as part of Regimental Combat Team 6 working with Afghan National Security Forces, a small detachment of marines engaged in a firefight with insurgents as part of a rescue mission to extract a captive AMCIT. Two marines were lost in that action: Sgt. First Class Vincent Ramirez and Lance Cpl. Hank Bindler. Two other marines and the AMCIT were injured. The enemy used weapons supplied through illegal arms trading. Since that day, the AMCIT, Jack Ryker, has worked in spite of his own injuries to expose and capture the man responsible for supplying weapons used against his countrymen. Gentlemen, Jack Ryker."

The guys stood with glasses lifted. Jack rose slowly to his feet and lifted his glass in return and looked each man in the eye. He was grateful. He stood because they knew about making a stand. They were the ones who had taught him about discipline, resilience, and grit. He couldn't begin to repay them.

The mood shifted, as much snickering and snorting accompanied something being passed around under the table. Nick asked permission to address the mess.

"Mister President, whereas Jack Ryker is a hemorrhoid and a complete dumbass civilian who wears his hair too long and has bad taste in tats, and whereas this same Jack Ryker recklessly lost his heart and, finally, risked his ass by taking off his hat and facing an armed enemy alone…I say he should be fined by this body. What say all?"

The guys answered with a chorus of "yeas" and a low drumbeat on the table. Miguel stepped up and handed Jack a Santa hat. The drumbeat grew louder.

Nick's voice rose over the beat. "I propose that civilian Jack Ryker, a real kickass Santa, be required to wear this hat twenty-four-seven until New Year's Day. And," Nick continued, "furthermore, that said civilian Jack Ryker be confined to the care and guardianship of one Mari Lynch. Indefinitely."

They banged the table, and Jack knew he'd passed the test he'd been studying for from the moment he'd chosen to go after Evans with a team. With a grin, Jack pulled on the Santa hat.

***

The conversation about where Mari and Jack meant to live took place in the dark on Mari's loveseat facing the still undecorated tree. Her friends had reminded her of the old-fashioned wisdom of not making living arrangements with a man before a proposal of marriage had been offered.

They were wise, and they were right, too, that on the surface of things she and Jack didn't appear to be a match. On the surface, Mari and Grant had been the perfect match. But the surface wasn't what mattered. Maybe Mari had come to the far side of the hill, had separated herself from her family not for Grant with his ambition, but for Jack, who made her want to risk still more.

She and Jack had been thrown against a wall and made new. Each had been changed, was being changed still, by the other's love. He was not "The Invisible Man." She was not "Sister Maryrose." Tonight, he wore a Santa hat. He smiled when she asked about it, explaining only that his team had insisted. She thought the hat suited him, the way the white band circled his lean face and the tip with its dangling white ball flopped over one ear.

Leaning back against the end of the loveseat, his arms around her, he'd talked about his team and admitted that he still needed a driver and a trainer, and that he liked having a cook. That was her cue to think again about how they could make something new—a couple—out of their old oddly mismatched selves. He found nothing strange about having a live-in staff, nothing odd about giving orders or delegating. She understood that those persons needed living space, which her apartment didn't have.

"I have other houses."

"You mean like your parents' house?"

"Or one of the others."

"Which others?" She had forgotten, and he wasn't really understanding her hesitation about his parents' house, which seemed to hold lingering memories and regrets.

"Palm Springs. Puerto Vallarta. Montecito."

She smiled to herself. Oh, now she remembered. He'd mentioned those places earlier. One more difference between them. He thought nothing of having extra bits of real estate here and there. He was like the titled lords in the romances she and Shanny had read in their teenage years. She reminded him that she had a job she liked very much and wanted to continue doing right in the South Bay. And she confessed that she loved her Strand walks and being able to hear waves break in the stillness of the night. In the end, they decided to live in his Strand fortress. She had a feeling he'd wanted that all along.

"You're sure?"

"You mean am I willing to have sex on that sofa?" she asked. "You have to let me do some gardening."

"There is no garden." He sounded puzzled.

"Exactly. But there will be." She slipped out of his arms and reached to pull him from the loveseat. "Come with me."

He swung his feet to the floor. She was growing used to the way he moved his body almost like a dancer, at times quick and fluid when he could use his arms, at times frozen in concentration until his mind could exert control over some specific muscle group. She drew him with her to the wall where they had kissed on the night when he'd brought her the tree. She understood better now how he used that wall to brace himself. There were perhaps some advantages to his balance issues.

He caught her drift, trading places, leaning against the wall, taking her by the hips and pulling her up against him. Their bodies met in all the places they were meant to meet, and his arms came around her as he buried his mouth in her hair.

"You smell like Christmas," he whispered, his voice a low rasp.

He traced his fingertips up and down the ridge of her spine, and she pulled back and cupped his face to kiss him thoroughly. When they came up for air, she began to undress him. He stopped her, guiding her touch to his erection, and she closed her hand around him, conscious of the way his strength and vulnerability moved her.

"I wanted this from the beginning," he confessed.

"I know."

He shivered as if with a sudden chill. "Do you think a person should accept happiness he doesn't deserve?"

"Oh yes," she said, gently lifting her hand. "If happiness knocks—" She worked the small black buttons down the front of his wool shirt. "—you open the door wide." She pushed the shirt off his shoulders and pulled it down his arms. "You let it in." She pulled him forward and tugged the T-shirt over his head, dislodging the Santa hat, then picked it up and restored it to his head. She caught her breath, distracted for a moment by the masculine symmetry of shoulders and chest and ribs.

"You lead it to your best chair—" She undid the fastenings on his pants, wedged her hands between the cloth and his heated skin, and shoved them down over his hips, then she knelt briefly to help him free his feet from khaki and cotton. She was growing breathless now, intensely aware of her body, but she wanted him to understand how love worked. "—you pour your best drink in a brimming cup." She stepped back and shed her T-shirt and PJ bottoms to stand naked before him in her desire and raised her closed hand, mimicking a silent toast. In this, in desire, she knew she was his match in every way. His beautiful mouth curved up, and she stepped into his embrace.

Chapter 21

On Mae Sloan's little patio, Jack's friends stood under strings of white lights while Jack, wearing a Santa hat, sat on the flagstones with the boy Max, an as-yet-unnamed yellow Lab puppy, Mae's mutt, who was simply called Dog, and Soldier. Jack was showing Max some hand commands to teach the puppy. He hadn't explained the Santa hat, but he'd been wearing it constantly, and she liked it on him. Mari loved him unreasonably at the moment.

It was near ten. Mari, in a chair on the patio, could hardly keep her eyes open. Time to head home. Tonight, that meant Jack's place on the Strand. He'd made arrangements during the day to move things from her apartment to his. He was good at organizing and turning decisions into action. She hadn't expected that of him when she'd first seen him with a frozen grip on his shopping cart in the supermarket, but that quality had been part of him all along.

Jack looked up as if he felt her love and offered her his quick flash of a smile, brief as the wink of a winter star. On the little patio wrapped in a garden of olive and lemon trees and lavender, Christmas came, just like that. She could feel it all around her. It came as a special gift of insight when she'd looked at Jack Ryker and saw the real man revealed by a Santa hat.

She'd arrived at Mae's after the final shopping day of the season, tired and distracted and operating on coffee fumes. Now a spurt of renewed energy lifted her spirits. At home there was a tree to trim and stockings to hang. During the day, she'd explained the concept of adult stocking stuffing to Jack in a series of texts. She'd been ready to buy him one, but he'd told her that he'd found his childhood stocking in Paloma's box.

Mari was wondering whether she'd found enough to fill that stocking when Josh Huntington came out of the house, bringing his fiancée a coat. He helped Emma into it and turned to Mari. "I'm glad you came tonight. You proved me right."

"Right? About what?" she asked. Around them, the others began to move. Mae took Max to show him where the puppy and Dog were going to sleep. Jack pushed up from the flagstones.

"Don't encourage him," Emma said, looking at Josh. "He thinks he's a big matchmaker."

"Hey, look around you," Josh told her. "Sloan and Annie, Ryker and Mari, and, of course, us." He gave Emma a hug, which she didn't resist.

"It was the least I could do," he said. "Ten years ago, things took a bad turn for Sloan and Ryker when they left Canyon."

"And not for you?" Emma asked quietly.

Mari thought Emma must have felt the look Huntington gave her right down to her toes.

"Maybe," he said.

"Maybe what?" Sloan asked.

"*Maybe*," said Josh, "my matchmaking was a way of undoing the damage Canyon did to you and Ryker all those years ago."

Sloan lifted one black brow, his arm around his pregnant wife. "We've made our peace with Canyon and each other, haven't we?"

"If you have, I have," said Jack, speaking to Sloan but looking at Mari. "Merry Christmas, all."

***

Two stories above the Strand, Jack and Mari kept the windows open to the night air and the sound of the waves. They nested together on the sofa in their living room as their tree stood in a corner, glowing with some low-flicker lights Mari had found, and trimmed with their combined ornament collection. They had competed in embarrassing each other with their childhood craft productions. Jack insisted that her pipe-cleaner, Styrofoam-ball snowman needed a prominent place on the tree. She'd retaliated by hanging a particularly lumpish bit of purple acrylic that purported to be a star at the top.

Then they'd gone their separate ways to prepare stockings for each other. He gave her his red velveteen stocking with its toy train applique. She handed him her blue needle-pointed angel stocking. He liked the idea that in the morning they would greet each other with those stockings. She had explained the tradition of putting walnuts and tangerines in the toes, and he hoped she wouldn't mind that he'd broken with tradition just a bit to put a small velvet sack with a ring in the toe of her stocking.

Filling Mari's stocking was a bit of what Huntington had said—an undoing of past wrongs. That's what Jack had been up to since he'd returned to LA. Perhaps the person he'd most wronged had been his mother. That night before their graduation, he had believed she betrayed him by having an affair with Headmaster Chambers. He had misunderstood her and gone off and left her. Now that he loved Mari, he knew better, knew that he was the one who had been selfish. He understood that his mother had given him her love even when she herself had been starved for it.

The ring in the toe of Mari's stocking might be his main gift to her, but he'd also put a wrapped dictionary from Shanny's bookstore under the tree, a real one they could both use. He'd looked up all the wrong words years ago. Now he was going to look up *happiness*, *joy*, *bliss*, *felicity,* and more.

"Worried about tomorrow?" They were going to church together and to Christmas dinner at her parents' house, a plan that probably would have terrified him a few weeks earlier.

"I want them to love you," she said. "It's unreasonable, I know. I don't want you to be uncomfortable or…"

"So, I should not tell your dad how much I enjoy sleeping with you?"

"Probably not." She laughed. "Would you?"

"Don't worry," he said. "One step at a time."

How he'd hated that whole "baby steps" concept when he'd begun to make his way back from captivity and injury. He'd come a long way from the military hospital in Afghanistan, where he'd first learned the extent of the damage to his balance, where he'd lain powerless, hearing Evans's voice in the room, unable to speak or move, knowing that Evans was getting information that would allow him to hurt more marines. Now Jack was taking the first steps, strides really, of another journey. He had a new team, a new self, a new understanding of the twists and turns a journey could take. There was one step that had to come first.

"Can we visit your grandpa on the way to your parents' place tomorrow?"

She turned in his hold, looking up in surprise. "You want to see Grandpa?"

“He may not understand, but I want to thank him for being my Santa this year and bringing me the gift of you.”

“I love you,” she said.

“I’m counting on it,” he answered.

She’d seen him brought to his knees more than once. Her love had lifted him up each time, and on Christmas morning when she opened her stocking, he would go down on his knees again for her.

Her “yes” would lift him up forever.

ABOUT THE AUTHOR

Kate has lived most of her life along the California coast. That experience has made her a jeans-wearing, toes in wet-sand, married to a surfer, fog-loving weather wimp, with a hint of East Coast polish from spending her college years in Boston. Family history connects her to Irish and English immigrants, Cornish miners, gold prospectors, and adventurers who sailed around Cape Horn bound for San Francisco.

When she's not reading, writing, or brainstorming, Kate walks in the redwoods, feed birds, collect books, apples and leaves. She watches *telenovellas* on Spanish-language TV and immerses herself in all things British.

Her favorite food groups are butter, brown sugar, dark chocolate, and red wine. Kate's early literary influences were *The Little Engine That Could*, *The Little Red Hen*, and *Winnie the Pooh*. Austen, Heyer, Chaucer, and Homer came later and inspired her to put that first plot on paper.

Kate's heroes are honorable, virile outsiders with some grand ambition. Her heroines are practical princesses, who drive those edgy loners into love with good sense and good sex.

Her family and friends offer endless support and humor. Kate says her children are her best works, and her husband is her favorite hero.

Connect with Kate:
website: katemoore.com
facebook: /KateMooreAuthor
twitter: @MooreKate0
instagram: @katemooreauthor

www.BOROUGHSPUBLISHINGGROUP.com

If you enjoyed this book, please write a review. Our authors appreciate the feedback, and it helps future readers find books they love. We welcome your comments and invite you to send them to info@boroughspublishinggroup.com.

Follow us on Facebook, Twitter and Instagram, and be sure to sign up for our newsletter for surprises and new releases from your favorite authors.

Are you an aspiring writer? Check out www.boroughspublishinggroup.com/submit and see if we can help you make your dreams come true.

Love podcasts? Enjoy ours at www.boroughspublishinggroup.com/podcast

www.ingramcontent.com/pod-product-compliance
Lightning Source LLC
LaVergne TN
LVHW090945080826
845145LV00003B/891

* 9 7 8 1 9 5 3 8 1 0 8 5 4 *